A TREATY OF LOVE

A TREATY
OF LOVE

A novel

by

Samir El-Youssef

HALBAN
LONDON

First published in Great Britain by
Halban Publishers Ltd
22 Golden Square
London W1F 9JW
2008

www.halbanpublishers.com

A CIP catalogue record for this book is available from the British
Library.

ISBN 978 1 905559 09 1

Typeset by Spectra Titles, Norfolk
Printed in Great Britain by
CPI Mackays, Chatham, ME5 8TD

For Salma

Part One

I

First she moved in with me, then we thought of having a baby, then my father died. We had peace, then we had war; peace and war again and again. But now she's gone out. Ruth's gone out to the post office to send a parcel. I saw her put on her coat, pick up a parcel addressed to her sister Dalya, open the front door and then quietly sneak out as if she was worried about waking me up.

She is out, and I'm sitting here having my breakfast: fried eggs, pitta bread and fresh vegetables – tomato and spring onions. I haven't eaten spring onions for the last five years. Ruth never liked onions, and now, absurdly enough, eating them after so long, the strong taste and smell make me feel free again. It's also a sign that she's not coming back, and I hope she'll never come back. I imagine her walking along the pavement, heading towards the post office. I imagine myself following her, walking behind her at a distance, far enough away so that even if she suddenly turns around she won't see me. I imagine her going into the post office, remaining there for some time – depending on the length of the queue stretching back from the counter – and then coming out, relieved. But instead of returning home she continues walking towards the end of the street. I stand there, watching her, her figure wrapped in that dark grey coat which she insisted on wearing even though it's not yet cold; the dark grey figure getting further and further away until I can no longer see her. She disappears – gone for good.

Of course if that were to happen I would have to go out and look for her. I would ask friends and people she knew if they had seen her, and call the few editors and publishers she dealt with. I would even phone hospitals and the police. When people disappear, even if you have wished it, you look for them. I would have to inform her family, her two sisters and brother; her parents are dead. I would phone Dalya, or no, I should phone Edith. I don't like phoning Edith, I don't like her, but she is the eldest and she's the one who should be informed first, unless she isn't available. I hope she won't be available. In a panic, she'll tell Dalya and Rafi, "It's what I'd always feared."

They, especially Edith, would probably suspect me of killing Ruth and then burying her body in some deserted park. Dalya and Rafi might give me the benefit of the doubt; Dalya was actually sympathetic to our relationship and Rafi didn't care much about his sister's partners. But Edith is a problem.

"How could you live with someone like him?" Edith asked Ruth every time they talked. "How can you trust him?"

Now she would say that she had been right all along. Dragging Dalya and Rafi with her, she would catch the first flight to London and interrogate me in her heavily accented English as to when and how Ruth disappeared, her piercing eyes watching my every gesture.

4

I have never seen Edith but I have often pictured her looking at me with piercing eyes, and sometimes, to make her look more frightening, I imagine her with bushy eyebrows, like two caterpillars stuck above her eyes. Yes, while she stared at me with those piercing eyes under bushy black eyebrows, I would answer every question of hers clearly and calmly. She, however, would dismiss everything I said as a blatant lie. She would insist on contacting the police with her suspicions and then, depending on the mood of the police, I would either be questioned, or the whole matter would be ignored. "The A-rab's done away with his Jewish woman – well, fuck 'em both!" the police would say, shrugging their shoulders. It's not that I have had dealings with the police and can predict how they might behave, but in the imagination of a foreigner like me I expect them to be outright racists.

Still there would be no trace of Ruth. Her sisters and brother would have to fly home. They have families and jobs; and besides why, they would ask, or at least Edith would ask, why should they carry on wasting their time worrying about a sister who had turned her back on them and preferred living with such an inferior being?

"She was weird, that girl." Edith would say, while Dalya would keep silent and Rafi would nod, probably not in agreement but in order to put an end to the matter and return home.

Eventually Ruth would be classified a missing person. And I would be free again. I'd be free to be alone, to remain in my flat alone, to do whatever I like, for example, to eat spring onions when I bloody well feel like it. But most of all, to be alone, alone until I die.

Unfortunately she won't disappear, not for good anyway. She will come back soon, sooner than I expect. I know her too well, she's incapable of leaving. She couldn't leave unless she was compelled to – leaving is her last resort. She didn't leave her family until there was nobody to remain with; her parents died, Edith got married, Dalya found a job in Tel Aviv and Rafi went into the army. She didn't leave her ex-husband until he practically threw her out; and she didn't leave her country until all doors were slammed in her face. Here, too, in London, where she's been living for the last eighteen years, she has moved house only three times.

Ruth couldn't leave because for her leaving was never an act of free will. I know from my own experience, I have the same problem. From an early age the thought of leaving, or even witnessing people leaving, made me panic-stricken. Whenever my family talked about moving I felt as if the ground was shaking beneath my feet. It was not that my family often moved; it was simply that my father kept talking about going away and disappearing. When, finally, I left, coming here to London, I did so only when I realised that I had no other choice. I could no longer hide, I had to run away.

Hiding for me was, and still is, the only way to avoid leaving. When the Israelis invaded Lebanon in 1982, I managed to hide for nearly three years, and I didn't mind that a bit. So long as I didn't have to leave, I was willing to imprison myself for days on end in one small room in a friend's flat. And when everybody I knew had left, friends, colleagues, the people I worked with, I hid in a shelter under an abandoned building. The Israelis had driven most people away and those of us who remained were either captured, sent to Ansar prison, or went into hiding. Most, however, couldn't hide long. Not even I, who didn't mind hiding, could hole up for long. There were few remaining places into which one could disappear.

It wasn't only the Israelis one had to hide from. There were a few militias and armed groups who were on the look-out for people like me. It was a terrible time to be a Palestinian. Of course it has always been terrible to be Palestinian, but in those years, between 1982 and 1988, I realised how appalling it could be. Fortunately, I didn't suffer for the whole of that time. I managed to escape in 1985, though things didn't get any better after I left – on the contrary, they got worse. Nevertheless I would have remained had I found a secure-enough place in which to hide. I like hiding. I like it not only because it's the best way for me to avoid leaving, but also because it allows me to be alone. As far back as I can remember I enjoyed being alone. I used to run away from home, from my friends and school, and hide for hours on end. I would feel so content that I had managed to be alone.

Ruth too liked to be alone. When she was a child back in the town of Netanya, she quite often spent many hours alone, in her room and also outside, far away from the eyes of her family and friends. She liked to disappear. Sitting with her brother and sisters, or with some friends, without saying a word she would sneak out and go to the nearby park. There she would stay until dusk, on her own, thinking and daydreaming. Her family and friends thought she was weird. They wanted to change her. They tried to involve her in what they said and did but rarely succeeded. When, occasionally, they made her stay with them, she was irritated, becoming angry and rude, so in the end they left her alone. We both wanted to be alone. Our fear of leaving springs from a fear of losing the ability to be alone. To leave is to go somewhere new, somewhere where it would take a long time to find one's own space and be able to be alone again.

Now, while I'm sitting alone in my flat in the afternoon, watching a black and white film on Channel 4 and waiting for Ruth to come back, I realise how much I've always hated leaving. Not just leaving places, but also leaving people. That's why I cannot leave Ruth in spite of wishing that she'd disappear. I cannot even ask her to leave because that would be as if I was leaving myself. Her absence from the flat would make me feel as if I myself had moved away.

No, I've never been able to ask her to leave, not even after I thought of killing her. Not killing her myself but perhaps hiring a hit-man to do it for me. We could plot her death in a way that would make it look like an accident; perhaps a burglar who killed her when she surprised him. Or better still, I thought shamelessly, we could plan it so that it looked as if I was the one who was meant to be murdered. I could claim that a fanatic came to my flat to murder me but when he was confronted by Ruth, he killed her instead. I was hated by Islamic extremists, I had received hate-mail and death threats, and so could prove that my views had angered them. But why hadn't I informed the police? Well, because I never took such threats seriously. Nowadays many people receive death threats because they express controversial views, I would say, but I doubt that they all inform the police. And so I would get away with it. Not only get away with it but also become a hero, a living example for those who are fighting for freedom of speech, and I couldn't help imagining all the praise that I would receive as a result.

Of course the whole idea was a joke. It was a pathetic idea which I had borrowed from a silly film. I never seriously thought of killing her. How could I have her killed when I still loved her? True, I wanted her to go, but I still loved her and certainly couldn't bear to see her harmed in any way. I remember how I had behaved only a few weeks after wanting her dead. She had a heavy cold and I couldn't bear seeing her so frail and helpless. Worried I took her temperature and covered her with heavy blankets, made tea and herbal drinks for her, and every few hours handed her tablets. I fretted about until she got fed up and asked me to leave her alone. "Go out, Ibrahim, go and meet your friends and just forget about my bloody cold!" she begged me.

But I didn't. I loved her still and couldn't stay away from her, even though she was only suffering from an ordinary cold. I loved her then but now, today, 30 September 2000, while I'm sitting on the sofa, watching a black and white film in which a man is strangling a woman in her bedroom, I wish she would disappear.

But let me start from the beginning. Let me try to put all these thoughts in order.

2

First we had peace; there was that notorious handshake between Arafat and Rabin, and then I met Ruth and started to think about making a film.

Somehow, Ruth's frequent melancholic expression and the growing inevitability of our becoming lovers, stirred my imagination. I hadn't made a film for twelve years. I hadn't even thought of making a film since before I'd left Lebanon. Actually I'd never thought of myself as a film-maker, at least not a professional film-maker.

I'd made only a couple of short black and white documentaries which were produced cheaply for the Palestinian Institute of Film and neither was shown. The first was thrown into the damp archives of the Institute. The director of the Institute had actually recommended destroying it altogether. He was furious when he first saw it. "What's this? What's this Comrade Ibrahim? We want films that represent our people, their suffering, their ambitions."

"But this film does represent all that struggle and ambition," I said, ignoring what he actually meant.

"Does it, really?"

The film was intended to show a typical day in the life of a Palestinian family in the camp: the sort of work they did, how they managed and what they looked forward to. But rather than the predictable parade of Palestinian families as representative of the whole people which was what the director wanted, I chose to make a film that gave the family the chance to talk about themselves as ordinary parents and children.

The father was a janitor at a boy's elementary school. "When I was young I was a donkey in my studying," he said, joking about his fate, "so instead of becoming a school teacher I became a janitor." The mother spent all day looking after her husband and their six children, four of whom were still at school.

The children came across as bright and ambitious. When asked what they wanted to do when they grew up, they all expressed the same wish and that was to get educated; that was also their parents' wish. One boy wanted to be a doctor, another an accountant so he could go to Saudi Arabia where "people work and make a lot of money", as he sweetly put it. The girl wanted to be a teacher, and the youngest at school, a boy of seven, wanted to become an engineer, just like his uncle who had studied engineering in Germany and was now working there.

Predictably, that wasn't what the director of the Institute wanted to hear them saying. On the contrary, that was exactly what he wanted ignored. They should talk only about our "national struggle" and "just cause", "liberating Palestine" and the rest of the rhetoric which meant very little either to that Palestinian family, or any other in their position.

"Comrade Ibrahim, is that what you want us to show the public?" he asked, and before I had the chance to answer he went on, "is that what you would like us to show at international festivals?"

This second question was meant to warn me of the consequences of my reckless filming. He knew how much I wanted to participate in these festivals and was telling me indirectly that I had made a mistake in not doing what had been expected of me.

"But I thought we had agreed from the beginning that we wanted to focus on the social aspect of Palestinian lives," I argued.

"Yes, Comrade Ibrahim, we want to focus on the social side, but merely as a representation of our struggle and just cause. Our society represents a political cause and message, like any other in the world."

I grinned and he didn't fail to notice.

"Why are you grinning?" he asked, clearly upset. "Is what I'm saying funny?"

"No! I'm not grinning at what you're saying!" I now couldn't help laughing.

"What, then? What's so hilarious?"

At that very moment, although he did indeed look comical, I was actually laughing at something else.

"You see, politics did come into the film but I took it out." I fell silent, waiting for him to ask why I had done that. I wanted to prepare him for a shock.

"Why did you do that?" he came back.

"Because if I had left it in you would have shot me," I said, wanting a reaction.

"Why?" he asked, worried.

"You see, when those people in the film talked about

politics they didn't say anything about wanting to fight to liberate Palestine. No! They complained about the Revolution. The man protested that the Revolution was full of thugs and that some of them came to his school to make trouble. His wife grumbled that the leaders of the Revolution were thieves who squandered the money raised for the Revolution on themselves and their families."

He looked shocked, just as I expected and wanted, but he couldn't afford to lose face.

"This janitor and his wife are ignorant," he barked, justifying himself. "They lack political awareness. They are just ignorant and selfish. They're only worried about their own survival."

"Well, they're a typical Palestinian family," I replied, adding mockingly, "perhaps the majority of the Palestinian people are ignorant and selfish."

"Ibrahim!" he interrupted warningly. Calling me by my first name without the term comrade indicated that he had no patience with my sarcasm.

"Well, it's your film now, and you can do what you like with it." I walked out of the office.

I don't remember feeling angry or frustrated. I actually didn't mind the sad fate of my film. The whole business of film-making was never a serious pursuit for me. I was in my early twenties and knew that I was still young enough to have a hobby. I came from a refugee background so I thought of film-making as something I would grow out of before settling into a proper profession, which meant being a doctor or an engineer, a teacher or an accountant, a mechanic or, if your brain and skills weren't up to standard, you were expected to resign yourself to a manual labourer's job.

However, by the time I had grown up our way of life had changed. The PLO had taken over, especially in the camps, and quite a lot of my generation felt that there was no longer any need to take up a "proper" job. The PLO was rich enough to provide those who joined it with an adequate income and many just accepted that. Nevertheless, traditional culture had hardly changed and becoming a film-maker was still not appreciated or even understood, not even by those who had by then become ardent radio listeners and television viewers.

Our home, for example, was one of the first in our street to possess a radio and, later on, a television. But my family wasn't interested in films. They didn't see my films, nor did they know that I'd made films. I never told them; I was embarrassed, even ashamed, to tell them. All they knew was that I was working in something to do with cinema.

My second film had no more luck than the first. I had barely finished it when the Israelis invaded. The Institute, like many Palestinian institutions in Beirut, was razed to the ground and it was only by sheer luck that a copy of each of my films survived. The fellow who assisted me in making them, and who was more keen on making them than I had ever been, had stolen them from the Institute and kept them at his home. He later transferred them on to video-cassettes.

Of course, I was relieved that they had survived but I didn't watch them again until many years later.

No, I didn't think of myself as a film-maker, and especially not after the Israeli invasion. Three years' hiding in Lebanon, and many more years of being an exile in London, surviving on state hand-outs, made me think of myself only as a miserable sod just trying to get by. Even after I managed to find a job, reviewing films for a small circulation weekly, I still couldn't call myself a film–maker. I felt film-making belonged to a long-gone past. What's more, the brilliant documentaries that I'd seen since coming to London made me feel so diffident about my two old films that I didn't even want to see them again. At least not until I met Ruth.

When she knew that I'd made films, she was thrilled and insisted on seeing them. She liked them. Yes, they were modestly produced, she said, but they revealed great potential.

"The one about the poet is really wonderful. The way the camera follows the poet in his quest for inspiration…"

She was talking about the second film.

"Yes, but the poet was shit, his poetry was shit," I argued dismissively, though I was so happy that she liked what she saw. "I made a film about him because he's the only poet who could get the director of the Institute to pay for it. He was on good terms with him."

"Still the film is great," she said. "Look at those images, and the camera movement. How old were you when you made it?"

"Twenty-three, twenty-four." I was looking at the screen, observing the stealthy movement of the camera following the poet while he walked through narrow winding alleys.

"Where was that?" she asked. "In the camp where you were born?"

"No. I was born in El Bass," I said. "This is Shatila camp."

"You mean Sabra and Shatila?" she asked hesitantly.

"No. In Shatila only." I replied, but at the same moment, realising that she thought Sabra and Shatila were one and the same camp, I added, "The two camps are near each other so it's easy to think of them as one."

"I remember when that terrible thing happened there," she sounded doubly embarrassed, first, for the massacre in Sabra and Shatila and, secondly, for not knowing that they were two different camps. "When I saw the images on television, the bodies of the victims, I rushed out on to the street. People in Tel Aviv looked stunned; everybody was ashamed of themselves!"

"It was frightening," I said but I didn't really want to talk about it.

"It was terrifying," she said, correcting me.

"I remember the way the Israeli public reacted; I mean 400,000 demonstrating in the streets. That was a tremendous reaction!" I said, trying to relieve her of her sudden sense of guilt and get the conversation back to my film.

But she looked as if she was totally beset by the appalling memories of those times. I wondered whether she was remembering the war or her life in Israel and, disappointed that she was no longer interested in the film, I stopped the video. I was worried that she might start crying.

Ruth was the sort of person who would cry about

anything. She would cry if she read something upsetting in the paper or if somebody told her something sad. Sometimes we would be watching television, the news or a documentary; I would look at her and see her eyes full of tears.

Her eyes were beautiful, so beautiful especially when they were washed with tears, but I didn't like her crying.

"I'm over-sensitive," she would say wiping her eyes.

But on this occasion, as we were talking about Sabra and Shatila and the huge demonstration in Tel Aviv, to my surprise, she didn't cry. I took out the video to put it somewhere safe, and she appeared eager to talk, to divulge something important, a secret which she had never before revealed to anybody.

"It was then that I thought I could no longer stay in Isreal," she said, reliving painful memories. "I thought it was immoral to continue living in Israel."

"But the demonstration," I interrupted, trying again to divert her, "what about that remarkable demonstration? Wasn't that proof enough that the majority still had a conscience?"

"They weren't doing it for the sake of the victims," she said. "They were doing it for their own sake, to exonerate themselves from the responsibility and guilt. They wanted to prove…"

"You can't dismiss that extraordinary protest as a mere act of self-exoneration," I interrupted again, trying to overcome the sadness and self-reproach in her voice. "Do you realise that was the greatest anti-government demonstration that had ever taken place in the region?

Don't you understand how important it was for people like me to see Israelis demonstrating against their own government?"

I was annoyed that she had become so emotional. After all, we were only playing at what, by then, had become our habitual game: she would attack her country, or her people, and I would defend them, or vice versa. It was a method by which we avoided sounding nationalistic and prejudiced.

From the beginning we were attracted to one amother because, unlike other Palestinians and Israelis, neither of us showed blind loyalty to our respective lot. On the contrary, we were always eager to express criticism and impatience with our peoples. I came to realise that adopting such a posture was the only way we could live together.

But now that the massacre of Sabra and Shatila had come up, Ruth didn't seem to want to keep to her expected role. No, she wanted to explain something about herself too, something that had very little to do with our relationship.

"You know, I always wanted to leave Israel." She conveyed the sense that once more she was reliving painful memories. "People always told me, you don't have to leave Israel. To leave Israel is to return to the humiliating past of the diaspora, and to escape the challenge of the present. But I never agreed with that, never understood it."

"Yes, I know what you mean," I was slightly concerned. Her voice sounded like an echo of someone walking away, disappearing into a mist. I didn't want her to disappear.

"I was just like you," she continued, looking at me as if to assure me that she was still there with me. "I felt I didn't belong anywhere. I was meant to be homeless."

"And that's why you are now frightened of leaving," I interrupted her. I wanted to assure her that I understood what she meant.

"Yes, which is a funny feeling for someone who believes that she doesn't belong anywhere, don't you think?"

I was excited that we were having such an exchange of ideas. I was happy because what she was saying was what I'd always felt, "It's funny but then again people who don't belong anywhere tend to cling to the place where they happen to be living. They are frightened to leave because they know that if they left they probably would have no right to come back."

She nodded enthusiastically which was what encouraged me to go on, "This is the case with people who lose their countries; once they have settled somewhere new, they are frightened of leaving because they have no right to return. You are just like us Palestinians."

"Yes, I'm just like you."

This conversation took place after she had just moved in with me. For a moment I thought of telling her that I loved her, that as long as she was here she shouldn't worry that she would ever lose her right to be here; this was her home. I wanted to comfort her, but, as I realised instantly, I was only being patronising and stupid; she was not talking about living in my flat, she was talking about something else. I kept silent after that. I left her to say what she wanted to say, to continue her reflections or to change the subject altogether. But she said nothing.

Sitting close to each other on the sofa, we stared silently at the blank television screen. We were looking into the future. Or so I now believe, now that I'm making these confessions.

3

First I didn't consider myself a film-maker, but then Rabin and Arafat shook hands, I met Ruth and I started thinking like one. There were so many things a film-maker could do with a handshake like that: he could start or end a film with it, or do both; he could make an historical or a political documentary, even a feature film, or, best of all, a comedy. He could also make a film about an encounter between a Palestinian man and an Israeli woman, a comedy or a tragedy or a combination of both.

Yes, I started looking at things as a film-maker again, and at the same time Ruth's appearance felt like the beginning of an unavoidable change in my life. With the perspective of a film-maker I saw that she had transformed my life, or at least had given me the chance to transform it, and although at first I was reluctant to get involved with her, I realised that if I didn't seize the opportunity I would end up like one of my small circle of Palestinian friends in London. I imagined myself sounding like Ahmad or Aziz, or even Hani or Salim. Appalled, I saw myself with them after work every evening in that pub in Hammersmith. I imagined myself gulping down pints of lager while we talked about the same old things with the same degree of conviction, not realising that our views were getting staler while our life was going nowhere.

Salim would start the conversation by complaining about his job, and how, generally speaking, job opportunities were getting fewer and less tempting, especially for those of us who were doomed to work for the migrant Arab media. Hani would suggest that we should go back home, but then would wonder, sounding as if he had discovered some new fact, if returning was an option at all. Ahmad or Aziz would volunteer an explanation for the political significance of our situation, an explanation which would lead us back to what we had said the evening before and, in fact, every evening before that.

"We and people like us are not here by chance," Ahmad would claim. "There's a new world order and things have been planned to be the way they are."

"There is a higher political decision to design the Arab world the way it's been designed," Aziz would add, asserting what Ahmad had just said.

Yes, imagining myself stuck in such company, I felt desperately in need of a shake-up. And so it was that I welcomed the appearance of Ruth in my life. She was the unfamiliar character whose presence I badly needed at that precise time. By getting involved with her, I discovered that we, my friends and I, were only pretending that we wanted to help our people, and that it was all the fault of our leadership who had ensured that no new blood should join them.

It was a lie which Ahmad repeated and with which we all agreed. "In order to survive, the old guard has kept us away; they had to block our way in case we managed to force our way in, hence the so-called peace process."

"That's our tragedy," agreed Aziz and the rest nodded too.

"After their many failures, particularly since 1982 and the start of the intifada," Ahmad went on, repeating the same old line, "the old guard needed a breakthrough. Oslo was that break, and it was meant to stop the new generation taking over and steer Palestinian politics in the right direction."

Ahmad never explained who he meant by the "new generation". He usually talked in a vague way, but now, after I'd met Ruth, I know that he was only talking about us, the five Palestinian friends, who met every evening in a pub in Hammersmith. Absurdly enough we believed that we were meant to be the new generation of leaders who, having been unfortunate enough to grow up during a time of disillusionment and ruin, had a duty to rise up out of the ashes and resume the struggle.

It was a complete waste of time, I came to realise after I'd met Ruth. And I told her so later when we talked about my Palestinian friends. I was trying to explain to her why I no longer wished to see them.

Ruth occasionally met her own Israeli friends and she thought that one must keep in touch with people from back home; one must know what was happening.

"But it's useless," I went on, "for years we talked, pretending to be part of the 'new generation' of saviours, but had we been given the opportunity to play a political role, it would've been a disaster."

"Why?"

"Because we wouldn't have known what to do. For example, how to organise ourselves, how to mobilise our society, and eventually how to achieve victory, or at least an honourable peace. 'We must support the intifada by all possible means!' Ahmad always declared and Aziz would repeat 'The challenge now is to make the intifada last!' The rest of us used to nod in agreement. What we never asked ourselves was how to support the intifada but more importantly to what practical political purpose."

"Yes I see," Ruth interrupted me, probably believing that I wasn't being fair to my friends, "you didn't do anything, you just talked. But that's something, it kept you in touch with your people, and kept you aware and concerned."

"But we weren't concerned, we didn't care!" I said.

"How could you say that?"

"It's the truth. We talked not out of concern but actually to hide our lack of concern."

"I don't understand!"

"Look, we talked about the intifada! But only as if the intifada was not a political means to a political end, but rather an end in itself, whose only purpose was to provide pleasure to those who either participated in it or just supported it from the outside. Since I've met you and stopped attending those evening get-togethers, I realise that the pleasure of supporting the intifada, or merely claiming to support it, helped us hide our lack of concern."

Ruth wasn't convinced. Or perhaps she didn't want to

be. So I went on "We were also hiding our ignorance of the political reality. None of us has ever been to the West Bank or Gaza, and apart from what we saw on the news we had no idea what the intifada was, who was behind it, and how it worked. We were just playing a game!"

"How could it be a game?" she protested. "You're all Palestinians and what's been happening must've mattered to you!"

"Look this needs a long explanation," I pleaded with her. I thought she wasn't going to understand me.

"Explain it then."

"No, you don't want to understand." I was irritated. "You just think that I'm being disloyal to my friends."

"No, that's not true!"

"Let's forget it. Forget it, please!"

But she couldn't. Later that day she returned to the subject. "Look if we want to understand each other we must discuss these things. You must tell me."

Now I'd calmed down and I actually wanted to explain, not only to her but to myself too. I too had suspected that I'd been totally disloyal to my friends and felt troubled.

"Look, the five of us were born and brought up in refugee camps in Jordan and Lebanon. We're roughly the same age. We came to Britain about the same time. We've all worked for Arab newspapers and magazines, and although working for the Arab media in Europe is not the most secure way of earning a living, we have, to various degrees, succeeded in getting jobs and settling down in London. Our attitudes reflect our success in reaching and settling down in London. However, when we talk about politics, we're different. We sound as if we are still living in the past, back in Lebanon and Jordan; our views are an expression of old attitudes and prejudices. Although we all hold British citizenship, politics for us means the politics of the Middle East, and specifically Palestine and Israel. The fact that we're in London seems to matter very little during our discussions. It seems as if our relief at being here is merely transient; that what in the final account really matters most is somewhere else, back in Palestine, or wherever the Palestinian issue is represented."

"Well, this implies that you've been feeling guilty which means that you do care!" Ruth rushed to make this conclusion. "You've been feeling guilty that you're not there, that you're no longer part of what's been happening, that you have managed to get away, leaving the rest behind to suffer all sorts of deprivations. And you've been trying to overcome this sense of guilt by repeatedly claiming that there has been nothing for you to do back there; that the old and corrupt leadership has hindered your chances. Isn't that true?"

"No. You see even this sense of guilt is fake. It's part of the game."

"You mean it's only made up?"

"Yes. It's an attempt to hide our banality and emptiness. We are men in our mid-to-late thirties with ordinary skills and ambitions; but we assume we are important enough to pretend to feel guilt at not being back there, supporting our people in their just struggle. We are Palestinians, we belong to a people with a just cause and therefore each one of us, whether or not we care one way or the other are notable representatives of that cause and grief. Feeling guilty is just a part of our 'playing Palestinians'. Back in the camps, we used to play fedayeen fighting the Israelis, now in London, my friends and I have been playing a game called Palestinians."

4

First there was that handshake and I was introduced to Ruth, then I thought of making a film, and after that my life started to take on the quality of a film.

It all began a few days after the White House Lawn ceremony when Ruth and I were introduced at a party given by an English couple. Normally they were indifferent to the politics of the Middle East and only feigned interest to be polite. But with the huge media coverage of the ceremony and all the talk about the prospect of peace blooming in the region (it feels more like seventy years ago now, not seven), our hosts could not avoid referring to what was going on, especially in front of Palestinian and Israeli guests.

"Isn't it wonderful!" our host said.

"Absolutely!" Ruth agreed.

At first I thought that she too was only being polite, polite towards both our host and me. I didn't see any reason for her to be certain that the signing of the Oslo Accords was wonderful. I was still a sceptic about the peace negotiations and the ensuing treaties; too many important issues had been dealt with too vaguely or had been left completely unresolved, a weakness which would prove to be perilous to the whole peace process. I wanted to ask her why she was so certain but then I noticed her voice; her voice didn't convey politeness but familiarity.

She sounded as if she was familiar enough with me to know how I felt; the fact that we belonged to the same part of the world, although to opposing sides, made it seem natural for her to answer for both of us. I decided to say nothing, to let her speak on my behalf until our host moved on to talk to others, which he soon did.

Then I objected. "Nothing has been said or done so far that could be described as wonderful," I said, my voice shaking, anticipating her disappointment when she realised that I didn't belong to those who were euphoric. To my surprise, she didn't look disappointed at all; on the contrary, she nodded in agreement.

"So why do you believe it's wonderful?"

"Don't you think it's great that Arafat and Rabin have seen enough sense to realise that negotiation and compromise are the only way," and for a moment I thought she was being sarcastic. "Don't you think it's a great achievement?"

"No, I don't. I don't think they've seen sense." I was gradually becoming less nervous. "Both leaders are trying simply to hide the fact that the situation has reached crisis point."

Again she agreed. "They were going nowhere with their policies and that's why we should see this as a great opportunity for starting again."

"No, I disagree," I said, and so we went on; she hopeful and me sceptical.

It was, by and large, one of those discussions where most of what was being said was a repetition of what had been said many times before by many others. I myself was only parroting what my friends and I had been saying every evening since the start of the negotiations. These hasty and vague negotiations, my drinking companions at the Hammersmith pub and I agreed, were just attempts to suppress new ideas and new leadership. The only interesting thing about the discussion, or indeed about meeting Ruth, was that neither of us seemed to be burdened by an awareness that we belonged to opposite sides, something which had never happened in my earlier meetings with Israelis.

Ruth wasn't the first that I had met. Though I was working for a small magazine and spending most of my time with my circle of Palestinian friends, living in London had brought me face to face with a few Israelis. More often than not they belonged to left-wing Jewish or Israeli organisations and most of them talked to me in an over-familiar way as if to put across that they were the kind of Israelis who had Arab friends, that they were sympathetic and committed to Palestinian rights.

Ruth wasn't like that at all. When she responded to our host's remarks, she wasn't trying to dispel the expected unease, or awkwardness, of a sudden first meeting between an Israeli and a Palestinian. And when I asked her the usual, "How long have you been living here?" her answer didn't bear the slightest hint that she had been living in London long enough to have become different from people back in Israel. Living here, it seemed, hadn't changed her; it didn't make her eager to show that she had managed to rid herself of old attitudes and prejudices. But, then again, she didn't have to because, as I realised later on, she had simply never had them.

"In Israel when people swore at Arabs, or complained about them, I never joined in," she told me later when we started going out together.

She was talking about her early teenage years, before she started to participate in political activities. "Some people thought that I was a dreamy Arab-lover, or aloof, but I just didn't like joining in. At first I thought it was because I had no interest in politics but then I realised there was no point in swearing at people you consider your enemy."

"But did you really feel that Palestinians were your enemy?" I asked, partly out of curiosity and partly out of an as-yet undeclared intention to make a film about her. I had had many ideas for films but none enthused me enough to prompt me to try to find a producer. The thought of making films again reflected my desire to change, my wish to get out of the world I was stuck in. But when I met Ruth I thought hers could be a good story for a documentary, or even a feature film: the story of an Israeli woman who became disillusioned with her country and decided to leave. At that point I didn't realise that Ruth wasn't disillusioned; she had simply never had any illusions about Israel. In spite of her dreamy nature, the early death of her father had made her immune to patriotic feelings as I came to understand later.

I went on: "Why did you consider Arabs your enemy?"

"It was only in a vague sense," she replied. "I mean when I saw an Arab from Ramallah or Gaza, I didn't regard him as an enemy or feel that he belonged to people who were our enemy. No, not at all. I wasn't interested in politics, then."

"And what happened when you started getting interested in politics?" I asked.

"You sound as if you are interviewing me for your magazine," she replied and laughed.

I felt embarrassed and wanted to apologise and declare that I had no purpose other than to get to know her better. But before I managed to do so she went on to say that it was only then that she understood the extent of the difficulties.

"After the death of my father I realised that there are so many issues, the occupation, the Arabs of Israel, the refugees… so many issue which I was never told about"

"Were you shocked?"

"No, I wasn't. You see from the beginning I wasn't convinced by the story that the Israelis were good and Arabs were bad."

"Why? What made you think differently?"

"I don't know exactly. Perhaps because my family was right-wing," she said and laughed again.

"Ah! You wanted to be a rebel?"

"No, not at all!" she replied. "I told you, I wasn't interested in politics. I wasn't interested in anything. I wasn't argumentative. I just wasn't convinced by what they said, only not to the extent of arguing with them."

I was puzzled for a while. I wanted to ask more but she continued by saying that she was withdrawn by nature. She had spent most of her time daydreaming and, as I discovered when she moved in with me, she was still a daydreamer. But at that party, where we were first introduced, we spent all the time talking to each other. We moved away from the noisy crowd and found ourselves a cosy corner where we carried on talking. She wanted to know all about me, about my family in the camps in Lebanon and how I had managed to come to London. She was really happy when she realised that I had arrived round about the same time she did.

"Of course, for different reasons," she commented, and continued asking me about my family. She was so keen to know about my past that at one point I felt as if she were a long-lost relative trying to catch up with everything that had happened while she was away.

5

First there were the Oslo Accords, then Ruth and I met, and a few days later I phoned her and she was glad to hear from me. But that evening, at the party, we had said goodbye without exchanging telephone numbers. It wasn't that our meeting was so casual that there was no reason for either of us to think of meeting again. On the contrary, we both felt that our paths were bound to cross again. From the moment she began talking to our host, when I let her speak on behalf of both of us, it felt as if fate had brought us together. But as if to hold back such a feeling, at the end of the evening we didn't exchange telephone numbers. We didn't want to rush things, or perhaps were frightened of accepting our destiny. We knew that we were about to take a big step and were worried. Something had happened, we knew.

At first I tried to get her out of my mind. She was only one of those people you meet at a party, I said to myself, but over the next few days I thought of her, I thought of her a great deal. I decided to see my friends at the Hammersmith pub. I had avoided them for more than two weeks as I was fed up with them, particularly with Ahmad and Aziz, with their self-righteous way of expressing their opinions. I didn't so much mind Hani or Salim, especially without the other two, and I actually found Hani, with his constant worry about losing his job, his half-finished sentences and points of view, quite funny.

I also liked the company of Salim; his obvious kindness and his unsuccessful marriage made me feel close to him. I felt guilty about him too. I hadn't done the honourable thing when his wife Nada had flirted with me on a few occasions. Instead of rebuking her as a good friend of her husband should have done, I actually encouraged her and even went so far as trying to seduce her, but I'd always blamed it all on her.

Nada was increasingly dissatisfied with Salim. She flirted with other men and it was said that she'd had an affair with a rich friend of her sister's husband. I didn't believe that she was capable of such a thing yet in response to her flirtation I tried to seduce her. I thought that seeing Nada would be a better way of getting Ruth out of my mind than listening to the views of Ahmad and Aziz. However, I couldn't do so without feeling even guiltier towards Salim, but still I rang her. She wasn't in, nobody was in. "Probably she is out with her rich lover," I said to myself, and went to see my old friends after all.

"Ibrahim!" One by one they hugged me, delighted to see me again. Salim said they had been worried when I didn't appear, particularly on the day of the White House Lawn ceremony and he had phoned me the next day to see if I was all right: evidently I wasn't in.

It was nice that they were so concerned about me although I feared that such concern sprang from mere courtesy, especially when it came to Ahmad and Aziz.

Nevertheless I was touched and regretted their welcome didn't last longer. Soon Ahmad and Aziz began their habitual round of analysis.

"What's happening is a farce," Ahmad declared, referring to the White House Lawn ceremony.

"Absolutely!" Aziz asserted.

But this time, instead of dutifully nodding and pretending to agree with them, I couldn't bear to listen. I started thinking of Ruth. I thought of her all evening.

"I, too, thought of you a great deal," she told me later when we started living together, "I had a feeling that we were going to continue to see each other."

"Did you feel as if fate was bringing us together?" I asked.

"No, fate had nothing to do with it," she replied, confidently. "There was nothing mysterious about it. We were both lonely and waiting to meet somebody but were too particular to accept just any relationship."

"Yes!" I confirmed. "We were lonely but we were not terrified of loneliness and were willing to wait for the right person."

She nodded. "But did you have a specific idea of what the right person should be like?" she asked, smiling.

"No, not really. Did you?"

"Well, not exactly. But given an earlier experience of mine, I wanted someone who was not too foreign, or should I say not too English," she said and laughed. "Somebody who would understand my circumstances."

"For me it was the opposite," I said. "I didn't want a partner whose background was just like mine."

Soon we discovered that we had both gone out with people who were either too different, or too familiar.

Ruth had had an English boyfriend, Trevor, who was the office manager for a large firm of solicitors. "Every time he saw me upset about something that was happening in Israel, he seemed surprised, or even amused at times." Clearly she regretted wasting her time on a pointless affair.

"Sometimes he tried to be supportive but he made it obvious that what was troubling me belonged to the past and once he even said, 'I know Israel is your country but you're here now. You ought to move on!'"

And the funny thing was, Ruth explained, she didn't get angry or upset when he said such things. She actually wanted to move on, to forget Israel, to put the past behind her and begin a new life in London. But how could she when she couldn't keep away from Israel? She continued to go back there every two years, and sometimes, when she could afford it, once or twice a year.

In an attempt to understand her attachment to Israel, Trevor began to read about the history of the Middle East. "Israel is so unusual," he told her flatteringly, "that now I understand why its survival is so important for every Jew. I sympathise greatly with the Israelis."

His sympathy was neither appreciated, nor tolerated, for long. They talked about the 1967 war and when he praised the miraculous bravery that brought the Israelis such an impressive victory, this was the final straw. Her father had died in that war and she couldn't stand anybody praising either the bravery or the victory of the

Israelis, least of all her English boyfriend. She told him to shut up, called him an ignorant prick and said she didn't want to see him again.

My own experience, on the other hand, was that of the too-familiar. My short affair was with Sanaa, a Palestinian girl born in Jordan who had grown up in Kuwait; our lives were alike, to the extent that nothing either of us said was new. What made things worse was that we were both trying to impress each other by attempting to sound different, but the familiarity of what we told each other made us sound anything but. And so our conversations petered out halfway because of the certainty that the other knew the rest of the story. Only the sex was unfamiliar but on its own couldn't carry us for long; it just wasn't exciting enough to compensate for what we lacked, no matter how hard we tried. In spite of our claim to be liberated and our dismissal of our society's values, deep down we felt ashamed of sleeping together without being married. In the middle of making love, she would look as if she were fighting ghosts. I felt I was being dishonest, I was taking advantage of her, it was wrong, and I simply couldn't do it any more. Naturally our affair didn't last long.

But with Ruth it was different. We felt both remote from and familiar to one another. There was enough distance between us to make us curious about each other and, at the same time, there was our long common history that enabled us to easily understand one another.

But, at first, I tried to forget all about her; I told myself that she was just one of those people whom one meets at a party and who could be interesting, or even glamorous, for as long as the party lasted. And when this didn't stop me from thinking about her, I decided that even though I really wanted to see her again it would be better to leave it to chance. Our paths were bound to cross again and it would be more appropriate for us to meet without a prior arrangement. I wouldn't feel I was chasing after her and she wouldn't think that I was too keen. After all, I justified to myself, she hadn't shown any interest in meeting me again. And why didn't I let *her* get in touch first? I would have been surprised if she'd done so, but, if she really wished to see me she could phone herself. Eventually I relented and decided to call her. But first I had to get hold of her phone number. I asked our hosts who, to my amusement, thought she'd come with me.

"You were standing so close that we thought you were together," our hostess said in all innocence.

"Oh, no, we were only introduced that evening." I felt as if my ruse had been uncovered and so, in an attempt to change what she obviously thought, I added, "You know how it is when people start talking about the Middle East, they can't stop."

Quite unnecessarily I explained that I knew Ruth was a freelance translator and that I wanted to ask her if she would do some translations for our magazine; it would be useful to give our readers a taste of what Israeli critics wrote about films. She didn't sound interested but I thought it was a good enough excuse to use again when asking for Ruth's number or, indeed, when talking to Ruth herself. But when I did manage to get through to her, there was no need for any explanation and she was obviously very happy to hear from me.

"I was so sorry that we didn't get around to exchanging numbers." She was clearly eager to hear from me and the fact that it was me who had made the effort to get in touch didn't seem to mean that I was keener than her. She actually wanted to ask me for my number, she said, "but I thought perhaps you didn't give it out freely."

"Oh, no, I'm not that important," I said, mildly sarcastically.

"No, I mean I thought you are a bit too private," she said, "just like me, I mean."

Not that private, I wanted to object jokingly, but I was happy that she compared herself to me. That she'd thought about me as much as I had about her gave me an unmistakable sense of satisfaction.

"I've been thinking about what you said at the party," she said. "You're right. We shouldn't be too optimistic about peace. The fact that a great deal of what has been happening is meant to deal with the crises rather than solve the problem can't be ignored."

And she went on but I wasn't listening to what she was saying so much as to the way in which she said it; she still sounded grateful to me for taking the initiative and this encouraged me to ask her out for a meal.

"Yes, sure!" she replied. "I'm almost always free, more free than I'd like."

"Why? Don't you have any work?"

"No, I don't!"

"Well, look, I tell you what. Let's meet and you might

41

not be free for much longer." I don't know why I said that apart from the desire to please or, perhaps, to impress her. I certainly had no work for her. The magazine couldn't afford to take on any more freelancers and, besides, the editor was such a bore he was only interested in printing translations from French and American magazines and not translations from Israeli journals. He was one of those people who were stuck in the sixties, discussing the avant-garde and new wave French cinema.

"Oh, really, you think you have work for me?"

"I'm not sure that you'd like the idea," I said, "but let's meet and we'll talk about it!"

I had to make her feel less hopeful so she wouldn't be too disappointed when she knew there was no work.

The curious thing was that I didn't really feel sorry that she had no work. On the contrary, somehow I felt content that from the beginning I had the advantage. It was not that my job was glamorous or well paid but, as things stood, I was employed while she wasn't. And as I'd learned from many years of unemployment in London, when going out with someone who was in work, I couldn't enjoy the power of deciding when to go out, where, and how often. I wanted to be the one who made the decisions.

Recalling the sense of contentment I felt when I knew that she was out of work, now, while I'm sitting at home, waiting for her to return from the post office, I realise that above all it was Ruth's vulnerability that made her attractive to me. She was pretty but from the beginning it wasn't her appearance or the way she dressed that I liked, but her eyes. They were such lovely brown eyes. And what particularly fascinated me was the fact that they looked as if they were washed with tears, as if she'd just been crying. Ruth quite often looked as if she'd just been crying.

6

First we started going out together, then Rabin was assassinated and I asked Ruth to move in with me.

We had gone out together for more than two years and enjoyed the idea of being a Palestinian-Israeli couple. People were curious about us, even those with little interest in the Middle East. We became the centre of attention and unsurprisingly received many dinner invitations while our own invitations were rarely turned down. Everybody wanted to know how we were getting along. Some, blatantly flattering, considered our relationship emblematic of the changing times and the dawn of peace and forgiveness in the troubled region but we were embarrassed by such misplaced reverence.

"It's no longer a major problem for people like us," we replied to those who wanted to know more, "we have peace now!"

Even on the day of the Hebron incident, we still gave the same answer, clearly and self-confidently.

"The fact that a fanatic settler went into a mosque and opened fire at worshippers," Ruth argued, while I nodded in agreement, "is proof that, unlike us, and people like us, there are many who are opposed to peace and willing to use violence."

"But doesn't that make it hard for you to be together?" we were asked.

"No, when you are genuinely for peace as we are, the difficulties in being together are no greater than those faced by other mixed couples."

We realised, however, that we were not meant to talk about ourselves the way any other mixed couples would. People showed interest in us because they expected us to reveal a different understanding, and to talk about problems that others didn't have. When we refrained from doing so, they were disappointed and consequently we were no longer of interest to them. Some actually thought that we were being aloof and snubbed us. Only a handful of friends continued to respect us and it was them whom we carried on seeing.

Of course, at first we enjoyed the attention and there were occasions when we didn't mind playing our respected role, especially when it proved to be of benefit. We were approached by a television producer who proposed commissioning me to make a documentary about our relationship. He said that he was planning to launch a series aimed at presenting the experiences of couples from different backgrounds or opposing sides and had chosen the title *Living with the Enemy*. With the huge international coverage of the Palestine/Israel issue, he was convinced that starting the series with an episode about Ruth and me would guarantee media interest.

We thought about it and Ruth said that we should go ahead; this was an opportunity for me not only to make a film but also to gain a foothold in the media which in this country of old school networks and closed doors was practically a no-go area for a foreigner like me.

"If you make this film, you'll be able to do another. You can't waste this opportunity," she insisted, but I could see her heart wasn't really in it. She didn't want to be in a film. When I first met her I'd planned to make, or more precisely tried to make, a film about her. I quickly discovered, however, that she was a very private person and couldn't stand the idea of being exposed to the public; I felt ashamed that I'd even thought of making such a film. When she said that this was an opportunity I couldn't afford to waste and that she was willing to take part in, I knew she was making a sacrifice.

"We agreed from the start that we would make no sacrifices, no concessions," I said.

"It's not a sacrifice. It's something that will be good for both of us."

"No, it won't be good for both of us," I replied. "It will only be good for me."

"All right, perhaps it will only be good for you. Perhaps it's a sacrifice on my part, what's wrong with that?"

"I don't like people making any sacrifices." I was a bit irritated now that I realised that she too was thinking of it as a sacrifice, "People shouldn't make sacrifices, it makes others indebted to them. I don't want to be indebted to anybody."

"What about you? You've made a sacrifice for me," she said, "you've stopped seeing your old friends."

She was right, of course. I'd got completely fed up with them, no longer wanted their company, and now, after several months of going out with her, I couldn't see them even if I wanted to. Occasionally I phoned Salim or Hani but I stopped going to the pub. I didn't want to tell them about her. The problem was not Salim and Hani; on the contrary those two might possibly have wanted to meet her and invite her to their homes to meet their wives. But Ahmad and Aziz wouldn't have liked the fact that I had an Israeli partner. For them every Israeli, especially a woman like Ruth, was a possible Mossad agent. They would have avoided me or, at the very least, would have been uncomfortable and felt unable to talk freely in front of me the way they usually did.

Nor could I continue to see them and hide Ruth's identity. It would not have been right to listen to them without protest or objection, merely to pretend that I agreed when they attacked Israel and the Jews. On the other hand to disagree with them would have meant forfeiting my right to be there. For this small after-work gathering in a pub was not meant to be a debating society for people of different views. We met there only to drink and express agreement over whatever was being said. I had no reason to be with them.

"It wasn't a sacrifice," I said to Ruth. "On the contrary, I was fed up with hearing the same old opinions. I was bored with them and wanted a reason to stop seeing them. And it was you who helped me do it. I actually owe it to you."

She didn't look convinced. And we never talked about that again.

Now, when I'm sitting here, making these confessions, waiting for her to return from the post office and remembering what happened over the last seven years, I

realise that I didn't really want to make that film for the
same reasons she didn't really want to. I didn't actually like
the idea of making a film about us being an Israeli and a
Palestinian living together. Nor did I want to be in any
film, or in any programme that would make me too
visible. Just like Ruth, I wanted to enjoy our anonymity.
Not that I hated fame or had modest ambitions, but
anonymity for me, as much as for her, was at that time the
cover under which we could do the things that we would
have loved to have done in our youth.

Ruth and I were in our late thirties. We felt that this was
our last chance to live the youth that we never had. In
spite of our obvious differences, we both grew up where
one's life was exposed to others' curiosity and where one
could not be respected as an individual making his or her
own destiny. Worse still our small communities were
always so troubled that they made us see them as even
smaller. There was little awareness of the pleasure of a
peaceful life even when there was no war or fighting. And
on top of it all, neither Ruth nor I could ever enjoy the
bliss of having our own space.

Now, when I reflect on the similarities between our
early lives, I realise that we both grew up sharply aware of
our respective political identities and suffered their
burdens. We had had no chance of living a carefree, even
irresponsible youth. It was as if the permanent state of
danger which had overtaken our world had made phases
and ages seamless. We were compelled to feel and behave
like grown ups when we should have been playing and
having fun. Of course, many people of our generation did

play and have fun to their heart's content, but they were considered selfish and insensitive and made to feel guilty.

Ruth and I only discovered that our youth had been stolen from us after many years of living in London. Here, in this tremendous city, we began to discover the life we hadn't lived – that phase of rebelling against our parents and their generation as a way of staking our independence. We even came to believe, rightly or wrongly, that our unconscious motive for coming to London was to rebel against the societies which had deprived us of the chance of living our youth normally. Our getting together, in itself, was neither a manifestation of the changing times, nor an act of defiance against those who still frowned upon mixed relationships. No, it was rather an act of solidarity between two people brought together by a mutual sense of lost youth.

Of course we didn't go to youth clubs or raves; we certainly didn't want to hang out with teenagers. Ours was a make-believe youthful life. Like two truants running away from school, we went to areas where we couldn't be seen by people we knew, areas to which we had never been before. We looked through the *A to Z* and chose where to go. Some of our choices turned out to be dubious or even dangerous, but that was exactly the point, to feel that we were venturing beyond the familiar, to encounter the delight and also the anxiety of discovering the unfamiliar: to be strangers, and exposed to the dangers which strangers face in a foreign city. We were so anxious to experience the sense of being outsiders that at one point it was as if we were deliberately exposing ourselves to danger. We were jeered at and once we were almost attacked by a gang of skin-heads, and on another occasion by a pimp who thought Ruth was a prostitute and I her punter. After that, we limited ourselves to safer places.

We preferred lanes and side-streets and chose to walk when there were few people around. We didn't bother about the names of the streets. Actually we didn't want to know the names; this was part of our playing at young strangers. It was enough to know how to get there: ten minutes' walk from Camden tube station, or the third or fourth right from Liverpool Street.

"We must come here in the early morning," Ruth suggested once as we walked out of Liverpool Street tube station.

And so we did. In the dim light of dawn we walked the surrounding narrow streets. Sometimes we stopped, approached one another slowly, and kissed. London was beautiful and we felt blessed that we were there.

"London is so big, big enough to make us forget that we belong to hostile people," she said to me one morning, tears of happiness in her eyes. "London's vastness makes me so conscious of how small the world we've come from is."

And it was true. Suddenly I felt our world was no longer divided between countries and nations, so much as two neighbourhoods, rich and poor. Ruth agreed and then wiping her eyes, said teasingly, "So I'm the rich Israeli girl and you're the poor Palestinian boy who's madly in love with me!"

"True, and now let your poor Palestinian lover take you to a poor café."

After a couple of hours' walking, we would have breakfast or lunch, or just coffee in small, cheap, secluded cafés in deserted lanes. We preferred it when the café was empty or when there were no more than a few silent customers. Our conversation was mostly an exchange of a few short sentences. When one of us wanted to talk for longer the other would keep silent throughout. Silence was an essential part of the emptiness in which we needed to play our game.

We walked in the mornings only. Once it was noon we had lunch or coffee and then parted company until the next morning. We were motivated by the early energy of the day; we felt alive and relaxed and went about bathing our bodies and imaginations in the refreshing morning breeze, playing our game to our hearts' content. Of course it was a film that we were making: we were acting out our own private film.

Then in 1995 we moved in together and all that changed for good.

We had had no plans to do so, knowing that the moment we started living together we could no longer act out our personal film but nor did we expect to keep doing just that. A film must have an ending: ours too had to come to an end, and it came about on the night of 4 November of that year. I had just come out of the cinema and had to write a review of a brainless Hollywood blockbuster. I had no desire to go home just then so rang Ruth from a phone box in the street to see if she was up for a late dinner. She sobbed, "Rabin's been killed!"

"When?" I asked. "How?"

It was all over the television but of course I hadn't heard anything. "Calm down," I said, "I'm coming over."

It was very cold and I thought of taking a taxi. Ruth didn't like it when I took a taxi. She thought it was a waste of money. She was careful about money but she also believed that one shouldn't do anything that would undermine public services. I didn't often listen to her but tonight I was anxious to do things that would please her. Walking to the bus stop I thought we should no longer live apart.

Her brown eyes were full of tears and she looked as if she had just become an orphan. This was not a new feeling for Ruth. She was only eleven when her father had died and she had deeply internalised the sense of being without one parent. If it took her a long time, at least longer than anybody else I knew, to get over the death of Rabin, it wasn't because she was mourning a great leader. Rather it was the orphan in her mourning the loss of a father. Rabin belonged to her father's generation; they had both fought in the 1967 war. Though Rabin had survived the war he, like her father, had suffered an untimely death. She would feel the same when news of my father's death reached us; again it awoke in her the deep sense of being an orphan.

Seeing her in such a state that night, and the following nights too, I realised that we must stay together. She kept crying and I cried too and then we spent the night in each other's arms.

The next morning Salim phoned me at the office. Salim and Hani were the only Palestinian friends I'd stayed in touch with during my first year with Ruth. They were slow to realise that I was trying to avoid them, and I myself didn't mind remaining in contact with this less-aggressive pair.

I also wanted to keep in touch with Nada. In spite of my relationship with Ruth, I still wanted, if only occasionally, to hear from Nada. I still wanted her to flirt with me. I would feel guilty towards both Salim and Ruth, and once or twice swore never to go anywhere near her but sometimes the craving for extra female attention was so unrelenting that it was very hard to stick to my resolve.

It was not that Ruth didn't give me enough attention. On the contrary, she was sometimes too attentive, but the attention I sought from Nada was of a different kind. It was the attention of an Arab woman, the rare attention of the familiar. For a long time I denied that that was what I wanted from Nada. It wasn't until a couple of years later that I told Ruth about it. Ruth had gone to Israel and I tried to go out with Nada. When Ruth came back I told her. Naturally she was angry and left for a few days.

"But why Nada? She is the wife of Salim, the only Arab friend you've got?" she asked when we discussed it.

"I don't know. Perhaps because she's the only Arab woman I've been close enough to, to win her attention."

"Did it have to be an Arab woman?" She looked puzzled.

"It's a bit complicated," I said and started thinking of cousin Maryam. She had died a long time ago and I'd always tried to forget her. I was worried now. "Before I came to London I never enjoyed proper, I mean physical female attention. All my friends back there had affairs but I didn't. I had only one relationship and it was more a friendship than anything else."

"Why? Were you shy?"

"No. I don't know." It was because of Maryam, I was sure, but I couldn't tell her. Now, when I have the courage to make these confessions, I wish I'd told her. I wish I'd revealed to her that I didn't enjoy early female attention because I didn't seek it. I was frightened, the death of my cousin in that horrible way made me recoil from intimate relationships. I wasn't just frightened for the women I might have had an affair with, frightened that they too might suffer Maryam's fate. I was frightened for myself too.

I didn't tell Ruth because I would've had to tell her about Maryam and I didn't want to talk about her. I didn't want to remember her. It was too frightfully close to home and I wasn't ready to go there yet.

"Where've you been?" Salim asked. "Last night I phoned you three times but you weren't at home."

"I was staying with Ruth," I said. This was the first time that I'd mentioned her name to him.

"Ah, the mysterious girlfriend," he said. "When are we going to meet this Ruth, or don't your Palestinian friends deserve such an honour?"

"What's up?" I asked, ignoring his question.

"Haven't you heard the news about Rabin?" He went on to tell me that he and the rest of the boys were going out celebrating.

"Celebrating what? Celebrating what an Israeli fanatic has done?" I asked sarcastically. I had already heard similar remarks from people in the office. "Oh, yes, I suppose that Yigal Amir killed Rabin for our sake."

"Well, at least this will put an end to this pretence of a peace process," he responded and I could hear the voice of Ahmad and Aziz behind these words.

Salim was not much interested in politics; the views he expressed were mostly those which he'd just heard from his friends, particularly Ahmad and Aziz.

"We have to be pragmatists," he added when he realised that I wasn't with him on this one.

"Pragmatists about what? Disaster? You must be joking!" I was angry. "I don't know what some people expect to achieve by this kind of cynicism. Let's face it, it's sheer cynicism, isn't it?"

Salim said nothing. He must have been surprised by my anger. After all, this was the first time I had openly expressed stark disagreement with one of my Palestinian friends. In the past when I heard something that I didn't agree with I would remain silent or diplomatically make a sceptical statement.

"I don't know," he said hesitantly, "but I don't think we were going to get a lot out of that peace process."

"No? And what are we going to get now? Everything we want, I suppose," and I almost put the phone down on him.

Taken aback, he abruptly changed the subject. "I also wanted to tell you that we are meeting to say goodbye to Hani."

"Why? Where's he going?" I asked without great interest. I was still angry and didn't want to let it drop.

"He's leaving London. He's found a job in Dubai. Why don't you come and say goodbye to him?"

Of course I would have liked to see Hani before he left London, but that was just what I needed to do tonight, to sit and listen to Ahmad and Aziz gloating over Rabin's assassination!

"I wish I could go to Dubai," I heard Salim saying, trying to change the subject.

Why don't you wait a little longer and we can all go back to Palestine, I wanted to respond sarcastically, but I realised that he meant it. He really wanted to go to Dubai himself, and at that moment he wanted to forget about politics if only to talk about his personal problems, namely his trouble with Nada. But I could spare no patience for him or his flirtatious wife. I was still so angry that I cut him short and went out.

I couldn't stay in an office where Rabin's death was a cause for celebration. I went down to the pub beneath the office where I usually had my lunch, but fearing that some of the staff or visitors to the magazine might come in, I didn't stay for long. I phoned Ruth who was still upset.

"I woke up an hour after you left and thought that perhaps the whole thing was just a nightmare," she said, "but when I turned on the television I realised it was real. I still can't believe it."

She started sobbing and I couldn't help but imagine her brown eyes in her small, rounded face washed in tears. I saw the orphan child of the night before.

"Look why don't you come to my place," I interrupted, and added after a pause, "I mean why don't you move in with me?"

"Are you serious?" she asked. She stopped crying.

"Of course I'm serious!" and to assure her that this offer was not made either on the spur of the moment, or because she was in distress, I went on to say that we should have started living together months ago.

"But I thought you preferred living on your own," she said.

"Yes, so did I, but..." I wasn't sure what I was going to say next so I asked, "Look, do you want to move in with me or not? Do you want us to live together or not?"

"I have to think about it," she said.

Within a few days we were living together. Our film came to an end.

Part Two

7

First we lived together, then the suicide bombings started and peace seemed no more than a short honeymoon. So was our honeymoon, short.

Living with Ruth wasn't easy for me. This was the first time I'd ever lived with a woman. I'd always preferred to have my own space and had never warmed to the idea of sharing a room or a flat or even a whole house. In the few, and mostly casual, relationships that I'd had, the idea of living with a partner was the least attractive. Two of my relationships came to an end when I suspected that my girlfriend was expecting me to ask her to move in.

No, I wanted to be free to be alone whenever I wanted.

I hadn't changed but the difference was that Ruth was unlike any of my previous partners; she was just like me. She wasn't very keen on the idea of sharing a flat with someone else either. Even when going through tough financial times she preferred paying rent rather than live for free at a friend's flat. Against our increasing desire always to be together we were both committed to the idea that each must have their own space. At one point we thought that if our love was worthwhile then we must be able to share a life under one roof – living together was meant to be a test, but in reality it took a tragedy, the assassination of Rabin, to make us agree to take such a test.

My flat was rundown. I hadn't done any decoration since I had first moved in nearly four years earlier nor had any repairs been carried out apart from those that were absolutely necessary. But that wasn't a problem. On the contrary it gave us a chance to work together and as a result to gain the sense that we were creating our shared place. We turned the dining-room, which I had never used, nor did Ruth think that we were going to use, into a study separated from the sitting room by a large, sliding, glass door. From secondhand furniture shops we bought a desk, book shelves, a comfortable armchair, a filing cabinet, a sofa, a large mahogany coffee-table and other odd items for the sitting room and kitchen. A new mattress and bedding were bought from John Lewis.

Ruth proved an astute buyer, especially when it came to old furniture. She had a good eye for the genuine and the solid. She was also a skilful decorator. Pleased and surprised, I watched her putting on old clothes and a cap, climbing the steps and working the brush across the ceiling and top of the walls.

"Where did you learn all this?"

She laughed, her eyes full of confidence, but gave no answer. Nor was I waiting for one. I was merely complimenting her and felt proud of her.

Within two weeks the flat looked new. We thought that was a great achievement and for a while were confident that we were always going to be happy and that we would overcome any problems that would face us in the future.

Sooner than expected we realised that living together was not easy. Being in each other's company most of the day, every day, we didn't know whether or not we ought to do everything together. We genuinely meant to celebrate the fact that at last we were united under the same roof. We talked, we cooked and ate meals together, we watched television and went out to the cinema and the theatre, accepted invitations for dinners and parties, and invited people to our place. But in between all that there were times when we didn't know how to enjoy each other's company, or what to do when we were alone together. There were moments of sudden silence, silence which bore the inescapable question: What's next? It was a question which begged the answer that by moving in together, we had taken the wrong step: this we decided to avoid as long as possible.

We tried to learn the secret of a contented shared life; to accept that these moments of silence were an unavoidable part of living together. We tried to relax, to take things easy, to learn how to enjoy small talk, something that until then we were proud we were incapable of enjoying. But every attempt we made only made us more aware of the question we most wanted to avoid: whether we had done the right thing.

Luckily there were times when one of us had to go out alone, when I went to the office, or to a film preview, or when she went to the library. We also tried to be sensitive to each other's need for privacy and the need to be alone. She would stay in the study while I was in the sitting room watching television. But we were careful enough not to appear too eager to be apart nor to admit out loud the fear that moving in together had been a mistake even if the certainty was there. Still we couldn't remain too close for too long.

Now when I'm sitting on the sofa which we bought together five years ago, I can freely confront the fact that we were unable to remain close for long. We should've confronted this, even if not directly. I could've written her a letter: "Dear Ruth, what's happening to us? Is that the nature of shared lives, or is it only us? Perhaps we don't love each other deeply enough; perhaps love is not the major reason for being together? What is it then, an experiment in the possibility of a shared life? If that's so, I must admit it was tempting but now I realise that it's hard and destined to failure because deep down we cannot forget that we belong to two different peoples with a history of conflict. Dear Ruth what shall we do?"

Ruth seemed to have been more aware than me of this failure, although obviously not to the extent of openly admitting it. For it was she who managed to break the sudden silence and give a soothing answer to the question "what's next?"

"We ought to put our experience to good use," she suggested one afternoon when we were at a loss to find something interesting to say to each other.

"How do you mean?" I asked, knowing exactly what she meant.

"We must do something," she explained, "we can't just live in a world of our own. Our relationship must inspire us to do good, to be creative and productive."

We were so desperate to find a way of relieving ourselves of being alone and yet remaining close to one another.

"You're right," I agreed, with little thought. "There are so many things we could do."

Soon, however, I found myself genuinely full of enthusiasm, and urged her to work on her long-held dream of making a fresh translation of Hebrew poetry into English; she had already selected the poems but needed the time and a commission to carry out the work.

"That could be a great achievement," I said, though only out of a sheer desire to encourage her. I personally didn't like poetry and didn't understand it but could never say so in front of Ruth.

In turn she encouraged me to work on a film.

"You have such good experience, you mustn't waste it!"

"Yes, there are so many subjects for good documentaries," I agreed, still full of enthusiasm.

Of course we both knew how difficult it would be to achieve what each of us dreamt of. Finding a publisher for an anthology of foreign poetry was extremely hard. Getting a commission for a cinema or television documentary was, as I knew from my own experience, even harder. We both knew that but couldn't afford to acknowledge it. To do so would have meant declaring our shaky experiment doomed to failure. So we went on working, she on her translation and I on an old script. Anticipating rejections, we nevertheless went on contacting publishers, producers and commissioning editors.

This went on for a few months, each of us encouraging the other that eventually something would turn up. But with every rejection we received, our list of contacts dwindled and less encouragement was expressed. Finally we gave up; she returned to her journalistic and commercial translations and I contented myself with work on the magazine, reviewing films which I mostly hated.

We attempted to ignore our failure and neither of us asked how the other was getting on. However, ignoring failure instead of facing it had a price; the sudden silence returned. What's next? The question hung in the air every time we sat to have a meal or watch a film.

Then Ruth made a suggestion, "Let's go on holiday!"

"Holiday?" I was surprised. Such an idea had never crossed my mind. The concept of taking a holiday was, until that moment, foreign to me. It was not that I didn't like leisure. I liked to go to restaurants on the spur of the moment and had learned to enjoy good food and drink but such occasions were never planned in advance. The idea of studying brochures in order to have a good time sounded irresponsibly wasteful. In spite of having achieved a certain security, I still thought, in matters of leisure, as a refugee. Refugees didn't go on holiday. But I was no longer a refugee, I argued with myself, protesting. Yes, family, friends, relatives back there, were still refugees, but not me, I reasoned. Why don't I enjoy myself, why insist on pretending I have no right to pleasure? Out of solidarity with those who were left behind or out of guilt? I asked myself protesting.

"Yes, let's go to Paris," I said to Ruth, in an internal mood of protest, "I've wanted to go there ever since reading Hemingway's *A Moveable Feast*!"

"I read that too," she replied, "but no, I wasn't thinking of Paris."

"Why not?"

"It's too expensive," she frowned, reminding me of our modest means. "Unless you want to wait until we've saved enough?"

"No I don't want to wait. Where else can we go?"

"Here, in England. Brighton, for example," she suggested. "Have you been there?"

"No," and before she could suggest somewhere else I added, "I've never been out of London."

"Really?"

"No." I wanted to tell her that I'd never before contemplated having a holiday, that when you've been brought up a refugee it's embarrassing to think of holidays, even when you can afford them. But I was worried she might imagine I was begging for sympathy. What was worse was that she would be eager to be oversympathetic. And I hated that.

"Let's go to Brighton," I said trying to put an end to the inner monologue tormenting me.

And so we did. We had a good break, one of many which we took, when we were trying to avoid facing the facts about our being together.

Ruth knew how to organise things well when it came to holidays and within two days we were in Brighton. It was spring and the place was cheerfully crowded. We wandered the streets and along the seafront, sightseeing and drinking. I preferred the drinking to the sightseeing, but it was the sea that made it worthwhile. I hadn't seen it since I'd come to England and it was with longing that I saw it now. Ruth felt the same, though she had never been far from the sea for more than a year or two.

"Oh, I miss Netanya, I miss Israel," she said as we stood there solemnly staring at that huge expanse of blue, reliving our past. We were both brought up near the sea; childhood memories of the Lebanese and Israeli shores of the Mediterranean flooded back into our present.

"What did you dream of, then?" we asked each other and were not in the least surprised that our early seaside daydreams were so similar. We had contemplated many things but most of all we dreamt of the day when we would cross the water, to Europe, far away from our troubled countries.

We exchanged memories intermittently and then contentedly fell silent. Silence now didn't worry us at all. On the contrary it brought us closer than we had been for months and it was as if we had at last managed to capture those dreamy mornings we had enjoyed before we started living together.

Still we couldn't admit to enjoying reliving those early days as that would have meant admitting that moving in together had been a mistake. Indeed we were so frightened of reaching such a conclusion that we were relieved when our few days' holiday came to an end and we returned to our small flat and daily routine. The sudden silences returned, more frequent than before, and lasted longer. They didn't cease until the suicide bombings started.

8

First we returned from our short holiday and then the suicide bombings started. Dismayed, we sat in front of the television watching the destruction inflicted by the Palestinian suicide bombers and the Israeli retaliation. What frightened us most was the readiness of those who were so full of rage and hatred (people described on television as ordinary Israelis and Palestinians) to see the bombings as the end of the peace process. Ruth and I had been sceptical about peace; yet when our predictions seemed about to come true, we couldn't help being terrified.

"These people must be going out of their minds," Ruth cried out.

"They are already out of their minds," I replied.

And we fell back to our usual reactions when matters between Palestinians and Israelis deteriorated: each would blame his own lot. This time, however, things were too grim for such a mutually patronising attitude. We were angry and it seemed that we both wanted to be less understanding: I wanted to blame the Israelis for the humiliating way they had treated the Palestinians even when we (and yes, I wanted to say, *we*) were making peace with them. And I knew instinctively that Ruth wanted to say that it was all the fault of the Palestinians who had blown themselves up and taken Israeli civilians with them. Instead, we wisely chose to keep our differences to ourselves.

"We ought to do something," she said as we calmed down.

"Do what?" I mocked. "Send in our army to separate them?"

She gave me a sideways look. "I doubt that sending an army of any kind would help," she said impatiently, "but we could put our own relationship to good use."

I recalled our last effort and was tempted to remind her of the result.

"We are living together, aren't we?" she said. "Couldn't that in some small way be proof that people like us can live in peace?"

Yes, we were living together but that was no proof of anything, I wanted to reply, but was in no mood to discuss our relationship. Instead I went along with her, "What could we do?"

She seemed to have a ready answer, "There are so many peace groups in London."

I *knew* exactly whom she meant, those mostly Jewish groups, pro-peace, pro-Palestinian, and all for the two-state solution. Well-intentioned, but totally useless, they spent their time signing petitions and sending them to various sorts of leaders. Occasionally, they organised a rally or a public meeting. Ruth knew how dismissive I was of them: indeed she herself was sceptical and had come across them only because her Jewish and Israeli friends in London were members and had often urged her to join them.

"All right, we're not able to put an end to the occupation," they admitted when they failed to make us see the point of their activities, "but at least we must protest."

"Protest has to be at the right time and in the right place to be of any value," Ruth and I would argue.

But in the light of what had been happening, Ruth thought now was the right time to protest. She'd been on the telephone to activists in one of those groups who were preparing a public meeting and she wanted us to go along.

"Protest is important now," she said, trying to persuade me. "Those who believe in peace must show publicly that they are against the return to violence."

"Yes, but protesting through these groups would mean nothing. It would just look mechanical."

"So what do we do?" she asked challengingly, and then added sarcastically, "protest on our own?"

"Why not?" I chose to ignore her tone, "It might be more effective than the usual demonstrations."

"You don't want to do anything! It's all right, I understand, but don't make fun of people who do want to do something!" Fed up with me she went into the bedroom.

But I wasn't making fun of anybody. I really thought that just the two of us demonstrating was not a bad idea. A Palestinian and Israeli couple protesting against the violence, raising a banner which said "No to Violence, Yes to Peace!" Ruth and I could stand outside the Israeli embassy and then move to the PLO office in London. Who knows, the media might be interested, no the media would certainly be interested. The novelty was bound to tempt news editors on the look-out for the quaint and novel no matter how trivial or stupid. And perhaps, I hoped shamelessly, this might bring us enough publicity to secure the commissions Ruth and I had fruitlessly sought. I was certain that a television producer would commission me to make a documentary, while Ruth, having become a well-known political activist, would be able to contact editors. We would gain enough fame to get our projects going. That's how things worked.

Now I'll make it up to her, I thought. I'll reveal my plan to her and she'll be as excited as me. I called to her but the moment she came out of the bedroom and I saw those brown eyes in that small rounded face washed in tears, I realised that she wouldn't be at all excited. If anything she would be disgusted by my idea and by me. And I too felt disgust at the idea and so remained silent. She looked at me inquiringly as I got up and walked to the front door.

"What?" she asked.

"Nothing!" I said, removing my jacket from a clothes hanger.

"Where are you going?"

I made no answer. I opened the front door and went out.

I went to the pub. There were a few people whom I knew. I nodded to them and considered joining them but no, I needed to be alone. I bought a double scotch and sat at a small corner table. I tried to avoid recalling the thought which had made me feel so ashamed of myself. I felt sorry for Ruth. She must have been puzzled by my behaviour, calling her, and then without explanation rushing out the way I did. What would she be thinking? I wondered. I wanted to be honest with her and tell her everything that I'd thought of. A relationship like ours is only worth having if we're absolutely honest with each other. I recalled previous relations, and compared them with ours now. I thought of other people's, particularly Salim's and Nada's, and felt lucky to have someone like Ruth.

Eventually I thought of something worthwhile. I knew what we could do. We wouldn't join one of the existing groups, we would establish a new one that would bring Palestinians and Israelis together and treat the two sides as equal partners. I thought this was bound to please Ruth no end. She would realise after all that I do care and want to participate in political action. I finished my drink quickly and went back to explain my new idea to her. She was so pleased that she forgot to ask me about my strange behaviour earlier that evening, and so grateful that she threw her arms around me and kissed me. "You know one of the reasons why I have always been sceptical about these Jewish groups is that they treat the Arabs as victims," she said.

"Palestinians are victims." My earlier worries that she saw it all as the fault of the Palestinians had returned.

"Yes, I understand that," she said, less excited, "but I mean these groups are so patronising. They look at Palestinians as though they're children who can't be responsible for themselves and their own actions."

I wanted to say that she was no less patronising than the

groups she was criticising but I didn't want to spoil the new sense of reconciliation. After all, it was my idea which we were discussing and I felt it would be ungenerous of me to contradict her, to pick on every comment she made.

"Who should we invite to join?" I asked, swiftly changing the subject, fearing that we might get into another argument.

"I don't know," she replied, a little taken aback by my sudden practicality, "there are so many people I'm sure would like to be involved."

"You mean Jews?" I asked as if to remind her that this group was meant to involve both Arabs and Jews.

It wasn't hard to find Jews who would want to join us. Indeed there were so many of them we would have to be selective.

"And Arabs too," she added enthusiastically.

I looked at her inquiringly. I didn't expect her to mention any names because as far as I was aware she didn't have any Arab friends apart from two or three who were acquaintances of her own friends. I assumed that she thought my idea was so good that it would appeal to as many Arabs as Jews an attitude typical of most of the Jews and Israelis I had known, and one that irritated me. Once they thought a certain suggestion was good, but basically convenient for Israel, they believed it would receive universal support. I nearly pointed it out to her but, again, didn't want to spoil the moment.

"Who are you thinking of?" I asked, knowing very well how difficult it would be to get Arabs, especially Palestinians, and Jews together.

"Well, Yael knows a Palestinian woman who's been involved in some projects for peace," she said, and after a pause which made it clear that she knew nobody else, "her name is Hala, she's from Ramallah. I mean she lives here with her husband and children, but originally she's from Ramallah. She must know some other Palestinians. How about you?"

"How about me?" I repeated her question as if to remind her that most of the Palestinians and Arabs I knew were either rejectionists or sceptical about peace, and that was why I no longer saw them. There were a few journalists and political commentators who, out of a sheer sense of pragmatism, expressed views in support of the peace process, though I didn't know them very well. Indeed until the time I met Ruth such writers were the subject of both criticism and scorn among my old friends. We even accused some of them of being on the pay roll of the CIA.

Still I contacted them, three Lebanese, four Palestinians, two Egyptians and two Syrians. They all welcomed what Ruth and I were trying to do. They said it was brave and although they would have loved to have taken part they couldn't, with the excuse that it would have been better if such a thing were carried out by Palestinians and Israelis alone.

"It's really their problem and it would be better if they're left to deal with it without the intervention of other Arabs," a Syrian journalist told me.

Such a view usually came as part of what sounded like a lecture in which the speaker explained that his support of peace was based on his pragmatic approach to the nature of the conflict. The explanation in itself seemed compelling but the attitude of the speaker was utterly dubious. Two people were honest enough to spell it out to me. They were frightened of getting involved in any group which included Israelis. One, a Lebanese journalist, feared that he could be prosecuted back home if he was known to have any kind of communication with Israelis, no matter how harmless. He had to return to Lebanon and it was against Lebanese law to associate with Israelis.

Another was an Egyptian poet who was worried about being attacked by the *anti-normalisation* lobby. I couldn't blame him for being so cautious for in Cairo in particular there had been so many vicious calls to boycott any act of "cultural normalization" with Israel that writers and journalists avoided even being seen together with Israelis.

"It's not worth the trouble," he told me.

Nor was I any luckier with Palestinians. I had hoped some would be interested but most were furious with the Israelis: "Look what they're doing!" one Palestinian writer raged, "after we agreed to stop the intifada and make peace with them, after we've recognised their right to have a state on our land, look at them!"

I wanted to remind him of what we, the Palestinians, were doing too, of the suicide bombings, but he was too blinded by anger even to listen. I hoped that he would soon run out of steam so I could reason with him but he went on, one moment talking as an historian, the next as a preacher. I got fed up with him and decided to hang up but at that very moment he started saying something useful. He said that although he didn't believe that a group like the one we were proposing could make any difference, he saw no harm in helping it. He gave me the telephone number of a Palestinian who had been involved in such peace groups, a computer programmer called Adham.

"He's from Nablus but has lived in America and London for many years. Crucially he knows quite a few Palestinians who might be willing to participate." He then reverted to complaining about the Israelis.

It was all silly and a complete waste of time but the next day I phoned Adham. At first he said he was too busy to become involved in a new group. He told me about the groups he had founded and helped to found. They were all impressive but eventually failed because some of their members didn't understand what ought to be done. He sounded as if he were the only one in the world who knew. And the more he talked the more certain I became that nothing good could come of him. I told him that I appreciated how busy he was and I certainly didn't wish to put any pressure on him. Realising that he neither impressed me nor was I going to beg him to join us, he at once agreed to come to the first meeting, but not to join straight away. He also promised to bring four or five other Palestinians. I was tempted to tell him to forget it, we didn't need an arse-hole like him but the prospect of him bringing four more people made me keep silent.

So we eventually managed to get together a group of people, not the one we had initially hoped for, but enough to claim a successful start. There were twelve of us: five Palestinians and seven Jews and Israelis, including Ruth and me. Adham turned up accompainied by only a couple of students from Gaza. The sitting room was too small for such a number so we had to open the door to the study and two or three people sat there. They couldn't be seen by the others in the sitting room so when they spoke their disembodied voices sounded spooky. This was funny at times and some of the group couldn't help grinning which was embarrassing especially when the discussion was far from humorous.

The Jews and Israelis were very skilled in the rhetoric of political protest. In comparison, the Palestinians, including myself, sounded hesitant and awkward, so much so that one of the Jewish guests would volunteer to articulate our views. Adham tried to be logical and authoritative but quite often he tripped over his own sense of self-importance. He was further hindered by the frequent interruptions that Hala made.

Hala and Adham didn't like each other from the start: they disagreed with each other and after a couple of meetings became bitter rivals. They were very much alike, both contrived to appear more important than anybody else. Adham behaved as if he was the ultimate Palestinian spokesman, elected by no less than 99% of the Palestinian people.

Hala, on the other hand, tried to appear accommodating not so much to impress her listeners, I felt, as to prove to herself that she was capable of being an accomplished public speaker. Sometimes she made me feel that she was only imitating, not to say mimicking, the politician Hanan

Al–Ashrawi. Hala was in her early fifties and for most of her life had looked after her husband and children. But now the children were grown up, she was left with time on her hands, and with the belief that she was too old to get a job. Voluntary work seemed ideal and for a time she worked with English charities but she didn't get along with the staff and was advised to work with charities which operated or worked in Arab countries. They were racists, she claimed, that's why they got rid of her. After knowing her for just a short while, I couldn't blame them. She was a natural troublemaker. Her constant fighting with Adham brought an end to the group before we could carry out one single action.

But it is true to say the group was doomed from the beginning. Hala and Adham's rivalry apart, most members were often too busy with their work or with other groups or both. Those who attended were either late or left early, and agreeing a mutually convenient date for the next meeting took far too long. In just over a year we managed to meet on only ten occasions. We did nothing other than meet.

When Adham decided to leave after five months it felt as if the group had run its course. Though he claimed he couldn't put up with Hala, the fact of the matter was he'd also realised that our gatherings were pointless, that what we did or hoped to do had already been well done by other groups. Predictably the two university students from Gaza left with him.

But where Adham had an obvious excuse to leave, the rest of us didn't. On the contrary we, especially Hala, decided to carry on precisely because Adham had left. But there were only two Palestinians left, Hala and me, and we soon had to admit that the group had lost its uniqueness, in being a joint Palestinian-Israeli group. We had to admit failure.

Ruth was heartbroken. She'd expected a lot from this group and had put so much effort into it. She did practically all the administrative work, contacting people, organising meetings and taking notes. She even tried to mediate between Adham and Hala. I, on the other hand, was relieved when the group failed.

Now, while sitting here recalling the events of my life during the last seven years, I can confess that I was sorry to see Ruth so disappointed but not at all sorry to see the end of that group. It wasn't only because I'd got fed up with Adham and Hala and the few Jewish participants who every time they read an interesting article in *The Guardian* thought it was their moral duty to give us a summary. No, it wasn't only that. The truth was that I was not meant to be a political activist. I liked to talk about politics, yes, but not to be involved in any group or political activity no matter how harmless or trivial. That's probably why, for years, I was willing to meet my old Palestinian friends at the Hammersmith pub. It suited us to talk about politics but do nothing. Not only did we do nothing but no doubt to excuse ourselves from doing nothing, we agreed that we were in no position to carry out any sort of political action. Our generation, we agreed, had been marginalised.

I simply didn't believe in politics. No, to me politics was

a complete waste of time and probably would lead only to grief. This was the attitude of my father and my uncles, aunts and cousins on both sides of my family.

I was in my teens when the fedayeen took over the camp. My father and uncles warned my eldest brother and me against getting involved. I didn't, not because I was such an obedient young man nor because I was convinced that my father and the older members of my family were right, nothing could be further from the truth. I have always believed that they were wrong, that their parochial, selfish attitude towards politics was part of our collective grief. Yet I never joined any political party and never participated in any action, not even a peaceful demonstration, because of what had happened to my brother Fadi. Like most of our generation, Fadi didn't respect my father's generation. He believed that they were cowards, that instead of standing their ground in Palestine, and fighting to the end, they ran away like scared women. Fadi joined the fedayeen and was killed soon after. It wasn't, however, his early death that made me accept my father's and uncle's attitude towards the fedayeen and political action in general, but the way he died. He didn't die fighting the enemy, he was killed during a clash between two Palestinian factions.

My father was right, I thought, after Fadi's body was brought to us. My father was right, I have believed ever since, though I never had the courage to say it out loud.

9

First Netanyahu won the election and then Ruth decided to go home.

"You know I haven't been to Israel for more than three years?" she said one evening, breaking the overwhelming silence.

I glanced at her but said nothing.

"I've never stayed away for so long."

"Do you miss it?" I asked without great enthusiasm.

She nodded. But I knew that she really wanted a break from living with me.

After less than two years' sharing the same space the sudden moments of silence no longer disturbed us. It was now the turn of boredom. We had reached a stage where what we said to each other was becoming so predictable that neither of us had a lot left to tell the other. Even when something new came up, neither felt there was any point mentioning it. Boredom crept in, and instead of talking to each other, every evening we sat in silence, watching television or reading.

We didn't quite give up and still tried to do things together. We were anxious enough to think again of getting involved in political activities and tried to revive our failed group. We invited some of the old members to our flat but only a few came and this time we didn't need to open the sliding door. We proposed discussing why the first group had failed and whether it was possible to start afresh although we knew perfectly well that the answers would not be encouraging. But, as Ruth and I argued, the suicide bombings and Netanyahu in power would be enough to compel those who believed in peace to re-group and become active again. However, it proved pointless. The causes which had led to the failure of the first group had not disappeared. Now that we were trying to return to political activity to escape boredom rather than out of hope, those obstacles became clearer to Ruth and me. There was no point, we realised, and gave up.

After that we did less and less together. We started to go our own separate ways, spending more time away from the flat than was necessary. The desire to get away, and to keep away from one another, increased. We didn't see so much of the friends we had in common, keeping to those we had made before we were together or, in my case, making new friends. That was not easy though, and I couldn't help regretting losing touch with my Palestinian friends.

I contemplated phoning Hani or Salim. But Hani had gone to Dubai and Salim would insist that either I visit him at home or meet him with Ahmad and Aziz at the pub. I'd become so in need of different company that I was willing to suffer listening to those two parroting what had become for me ridiculous views. Then again if I visited Salim's home, Nada's flirting was, I thought, still less insufferable than the talk of Ahmad and Aziz.

In the end I went nowhere and saw nobody.

It had become clear that we needed a break from each

other and it was then that Ruth decided to go home.

"You know Dalya and Rafi are angry with me," she said, "they're used to seeing me at least once a year. But now it's been so long they suspect that something is wrong."

"Do they think that I'm stopping you from going?"

"Dalya and Rafi don't, but Edith might." Her bluntness annoyed me.

"You shouldn't have told her about me."

"And keep our relationship secret?"

"You did for two years."

She hadn't. She told them she had a partner but always avoided saying much about me so they wouldn't guess I was Palestinian. I didn't like it but I couldn't protest. I myself had kept her identity secret from my family, colleagues and old friends, and I thought we were even. But then, after two years she went and put her siblings in the picture. Rafi and Dalya didn't much mind. Actually Dalya was sympathetic. It was Edith who objected, "You'd do anything just to humiliate us, wouldn't you?" she yelled at Ruth. Ruth was hurt and for months they didn't talk to each other.

Realising how Ruth felt I tried to show some understanding for her decision to go to Israel. There were so many things I wanted to say but words wouldn't come out: I know you want to go because of what's been happening to us. For nearly four years you haven't been because you were happy with me, you no longer needed to go home regularly because our relationship provided you with the warmth which you sought in those visits, but now you are bored. I wanted to say all this but I couldn't. I wasn't ready to confront the truth that perhaps our relationship was a mistake, or at least that I had failed to make her happy.

I was sad that she'd decided to go, but now, today 30 September 2000, three years after she went to Israel I know that I wasn't sad enough to try to stop her. On the contrary I gradually felt a sense of relief and then actually wanted her to go. I wanted to be alone again, to become my old self, I must have wanted her to leave for good.

Yes, I wanted her to go, and I took her to Heathrow airport myself as if to make sure that she'd gone. Avoiding each other's eyes, we hurriedly hugged and kissed as if we were worried that she might miss the flight. We were clearly eager to part, at least I was. The moment she went through passport control, I felt liberated. Now I can do whatever I wish, I said to myself, and as if to prove it I didn't leave the airport right away. I wandered around, bought things I had no use for, sat in a café and had a big slice of cake and a pot of black coffee. Then I left the airport and went to town. I was nearly forty years old but I behaved like a teenager bunking off school and when I returned to the flat it was just as if my parents had gone out for the evening, leaving me the place. I could do whatever I wanted without the slightest inhibition or embarrassment.

I decided to watch a blue movie, something which Ruth hated. She believed that pornography was a prime example of male violence towards women. In spite of her rhetoric, she wasn't exactly a hard-headed feminist, but when it came to issues of a woman's image she became less tolerant. That was why, until only two days ago, I'd kept the story of my cousin Maryam a secret from her. She would have become wary of me; viewed me with suspicion. Not that I had any responsibility for Maryam's fate but my not challenging my family's silence would have made me no less guilty in Ruth's eyes. When I eventually revealed the secret to her, that was the end of our relationship. But I shall come to that later.

Ruth often referred to male violence, and no doubt that's what made our love-making less enjoyable. Yes, physically we were not terribly compatible, but we could, or at least thought we could, have satisfactory sex. We didn't want to admit that we were both too self-conscious to be able to do whatever we liked with each other. I tried things that I'd seen in films but she immediately looked uncomfortable and even worried so I stopped. She didn't like sexual fantasies and I was careful not to do anything that might offend her. Our love making stuck to the most simple and predictable pattern: we cuddled, kissed, undressed, she lay on her back, I lay on top, I penetrated her, we kissed until we came, or I came first and then helped her to come. Sometimes we stopped, not feeling the desire to finish.

No, Ruth didn't like sexual fantasies and I couldn't watch pornography in front of her. The funny thing was that now, after she'd gone to Israel, I didn't feel like watching it either. I switched on the television, put on a video, forwarded it to a scene which I'd thought very exciting but after only a few minutes I stopped it. I wanted sex, not porn, and considered masturbating but realised that was as silly as watching porn.

I decided to get in touch with Nada. Yes, I said to myself, Nada is the perfect woman to have sex with but without the risk of trouble afterwards.

That very evening, pretending that I wanted to talk to Salim, I phoned Nada. She knew that I didn't want to talk to Salim and, more surprisingly, she seemed to realise that it wasn't flirting only that I wanted. Sex was on her mind as much as it was on mine, the cow, and for an instant I thought of hanging up. "Has your English girlfriend left you, then?" she asked, mockingly.

Like Salim, Nada had assumed that Ruth was English, a stuck-up English woman, who didn't like me to mix with them. She felt sorry for me but believed sooner or later I would leave Ruth and return to her.

"As good as," I responded.

"Why?"

"Different cultures," I said sarcastically, "as you and your husband keep saying!"

"It's true, isn't it?"

"Yeh! Can I speak to Salim?"

"He's not home tonight," she then added mischievously, "but you know that!"

"Yes I know." I laughed in order to hide my embarrassment.

"Still, I can't go out tonight," she said in an amazingly straightforward and innocent voice. "I can't get a baby-sitter at such short notice."

"All right. How about tomorrow?"

"Salim's at home. After tomorrow would be all right."

I was disappointed and was strongly tempted to tell her to forget it.

"Anyway, tomorrow I'm busy too," I said. "Yes, let's make it the day after tomorrow."

I wasn't very busy the next day. I only had to attend a film preview, go to the office to write about it and then go home, unless of course I was unlucky and had to see the editor too. I would have to suffer listening to him moaning for at least half an hour. He complained mostly about how Hollywood had ruined the art of cinema or if not that, about the lack of new subscriptions. I pretended to be busy only to make Nada realise that I wasn't that desperate to see her. I knew that she could see me right away, if she'd wanted, but she was playing hard to get.

Teasing bitch, I said to myself, and nearly phoned her back to tell her to forget it. I'd already started to feel bad. I'd taken Ruth to the airport and here I was, a few hours later scheming to cheat on her, and not only cheat on her but do so with the wife of a friend. Now how would I feel if Ruth had thought of cheating on me with Salim? But the question sounded too absurd to be a moral challenge; Ruth cheating on me with Salim? I burst out laughing. I couldn't imagine her sleeping with Salim. I couldn't imagine any woman cheating on her partner with Salim. I laughed. But what if she cheated on me with someone else, someone more plausible? It wasn't impssible. Back in Israel, she had so many male friends, even ex-boyfriends. She'd had an affair when she was married, so why shouldn't she now?

I grew jealous, picturing her arriving at her sister's,

reaching for the phone and contacting an old boyfriend. I could imagine her flirting with him and then arranging to meet him. I bet her sister's phone is busy right now, I said to myself – she's ringing her old boyfriend. As if to prove my suspicions I picked up the receiver and dialled the number.

She was staying with Dalya; I didn't feel shy about getting in touch with her there. Had she been staying with Edith, I would have had to think twice. I wouldn't have expected Edith to be rude or unfriendly, but the fact that she was against our relationship was inhibiting. Ruth usually stayed with her eldest sister but since we'd been together, and after Edith made her views about us clear, she decided to stay with Dalya where I could contact her whenever I liked.

Dalya replied.

"Ibrahim!" She was very nice and told me that Ruth was sleeping. "She's been asleep since the moment she got here."

"Fine, I just wanted to make sure she's arrived safely!" I said.

"She was going to phone you herself but she thought she'd better leave it until she had a rest." Dalya then added teasingly, "You happy lovers you can't bear to be apart for a moment!"

Happy lovers, what happy lovers? What are you talking about? I wanted to reply but instead said, "You know how it is."

I was pleased to hear her describe us as "happy lovers" even though it was the least accurate description. But I was pleased that her family hadn't realised that we had started to get bored with one another. It was also good, I calculated, because that would make Ruth embarrassed about cheating on me or even about getting in touch with an old boyfriend.

"What! You have a partner in London and the first thing you do the moment you arrive is to go out with another man? What kind of a woman are you?" I imagined Dalya yelling at Ruth.

Yes, we were still very much in love I would assure Dalya, if only to make Ruth feel ashamed of trying to deceive me.

I phoned her the next day and the day after; the first day I phoned twice and the second three times. Ruth was happy. She had felt that I was pleased that she'd gone away but now she seemed to realise that no sooner had she left, I was lonely and missed her terribly.

"I miss you too!" she said soothingly. "I wish I'd stayed with you."

But then with all the questions that I asked her every time I phoned, "Where did you go? With whom? Who's he?" she realised that I wasn't asking her because I cared, because I loved her, but because I suspected her of jumping into bed with one of her old boyfriends. Naturally she was upset but rather than confronting my suspicions she kept reminding me of the telephone bill.

"I don't want to come back to find us broke," she said jokingly, trying to suppress her anger.

I was so eaten up by jealousy that I didn't care and persisted in phoning and asking her all those accusatory questions until eventually she could no longer control her temper. "Yes I'm sleeping with an old friend," she shouted at me, "no, actually I'm sleeping with all my old friends, one every day, sometimes two. Now, could you stop phoning unless it's necessary or perhaps you feel that you're really missing me?"

I tried to defend myself but there was no point. She'd discovered the real motive behind my calls and I stopped phoning, though I was still suspicious and jealous. To subdue these feelings I started thinking of her return. She'll come back to me, I said to myself, she'll be mine again no matter who she's fucked back there.

She'll be mine, I assured myself but I was far from convinced. Yes, she'll come back and we'll be together again but I felt little enthusiasm at this thought. Yes, we'll be together, but then what? Enjoy getting bored together again? Yes, we'll have the time of our life getting more and more bored, and for hours I could think of nothing but the fact that the eagerly awaited return of Ruth would only revive the boredom which had infected our life together.

Then Nada came to my mind again. My date with her that evening seemed the only thing to look forward to. During the two days I was obsessed by thoughts of what Ruth had been up to I had also thought about sleeping with Nada. Here I was, interrogating Ruth about who she was going to see while I had my own cheating scheme. I wasn't fair, I wasn't consistent, and the lack of consistency, rather than the lack of fairness, had always made me angry. I was suspicious of Ruth and angry at myself. But now I realised that there was only boredom to suffer when she came back, the idea of meeting Nada didn't sound too disloyal or shameful. Yes, I shall see Nada tonight and enjoy myself before I go back to my increasingly dull life with Ruth.

I got on with finishing my work. The NFT was running a season of old, tedious films by that pretentious Godard and my editor wanted a review from me. God, I hate Godard, I hate the editor, I said to myself, and was about to leave the flat when the phone rang. That couldn't happen in a Godard film, could it? I wondered.

It was Ruth. She was in tears. I couldn't help seeing her face and tear-washed eyes.

She was sorry, she said, that she had spoken to me so harshly.

"Don't worry. Don't worry. It was my fault," I interrupted, trying to calm her down. "It was my fault. I was stupidly suspicious, it was my fault!"

"Yes, but I've been so harsh," she said, "and it wasn't all your fault anyway. Things haven't been going very well between us and it's understandable that you should be jealous but, look, we can talk about it when I'm back. I just want to say I'm sorry and I love you."

"And I love you too, and miss you," I said, slightly hesitantly as if I didn't mean it. But no, I meant it. I actually missed her.

"I just want to say that things are different around here, I feel differently about everything," she said, "I mean things are bad but I feel more confident. And I'm sure it's because of you, of our living together. Look I'll tell you all about it when I come back."

"Yes, I shall be waiting for you." Though I was far from sure that what she was going to tell me would make our life exciting again, I was, nevertheless, happy to hear what she said. "I shall be waiting for you," I promised, ending the phone call. And before I left the flat, I phoned Nada and told her that I was going to be busy that night and for the rest of the week.

"How about next week?" she asked, sounding very disappointed.

"My English girlfriend is coming back!" With relief I hung up.

Things don't happen this way in a Godard film, do they? I thought, and went to see two of his tedious films.

10

First she came back, she told me a secret and I told her a secret, then she left.

At first, I eagerly awaited for her to return from Israel – or so I believed then. I had been happy to hear her say that our living together had made a huge difference in the way she now saw her country and I wanted her to tell me more. Then I realised that I'd actually missed her. I missed her terribly.

In the three weeks she was away I was very lonely. I knew that I no longer liked being on my own. The pleasure of solitude which I'd enjoyed before I'd met her was no longer attainable. Nor did I find solace in the company of friends, old or new. There was no point in trying to see old friends, now that Ruth was away. There was no need to suffer the company of those with whom I came to have less and less in common. True, I'd considered meeting them, but only to escape the boredom which had infected our life.

As for our current friends, I met some of them a couple of times. They were quite pleasant and treated me just the same as when Ruth and I saw them together. But I soon realised that I was not meant to see them on my own. They were not my friends alone and most of them were in couples who usually met up with other couples. During the two evenings I spent with them in spite of their kindness and attempt to make me forget that Ruth was away, I didn't fit. Sitting with them without Ruth made me feel like an intruder.

I stopped going out to see friends and instead decided to busy myself with my own work. I considered the idea of another film; the failure of my two early attempts should not prevent me from trying again. I reminded myself of all those great film-makers who suffered many rejections and failures before they eventually made it.

Perhaps I was just being foolishly optimistic but nevertheless I began work on a script which was inspired by my life with Ruth. It was about a radical young thinker who believes that to discover what is true about society and politics he mustn't be distracted by emotional or social ties. Reluctantly, however, he gets involved with a woman and soon she is pregnant. Realising that his vocation as a searcher for truth is over, he is forced to take on odd jobs to support wife and child. He continues to lament the ruin of his ambition to produce some original thoughts and, predictably enough, he blames it all on his wife. Ground down by his constant moaning she takes the child and disappears. At first he feels happy. He is free again – free to be in his world of ideas. He starts working on an essay on the possibilities of organising civil protest movements in societies riddled with violence. But halfway through he sees his writing for what it is, a lot of nonsense, and misses his wife and child and wishes they were back. He recognises that he loves his wife, he actually enjoys family life. More strikingly he discovers that he was meant to be a family man not a thinker – that was only a youthful ambition. But it's too late. His wife has moved on and he's left with regret at wasting an opportunity for happiness. He's depressed for weeks, starts drinking heavily but at the end he begins to entertain the hope of meeting another woman and becoming a family man again.

Foolish idea, I know now, but at that time I was so enthusiastic about this script that I couldn't think about anything else. I imagined it as our own story, Ruth and me. I liked the idea of picturing our relationship in terms of a story and a film. It made me feel that our life together was regaining the sense of excitement which had been waning. It was like reliving the start of the relationship. We were deemed to be the script for a film, and what I was writing was its core. I kept working and by the time Ruth returned I was nearly at the end. I had decided not to tell her about the script until it was completed but on the day of her return I went to the airport to pick her up and on the way back I blurted it out.

"So, we both have something new in our lives," she paused. "This break has done us a lot of good."

I knew that she was trying to remind me of what she'd told me on the telephone. She too had something to say and had wanted to tell me about it before I launched into my script. She must have felt that I was not interested in her news. Having written this script, I had become, I must admit, less eager to hear what she wished to say. I was less keen to hear or to know anything. I was no longer worried that boredom would take over the moment we were together again. Still I pretended to be curious, and the moment we arrived home I asked her all about her trip.

"Things are bad in Israel," she said, "I mean they're worse than before. Or perhaps because I haven't been there for three years they're the same but this time they looked worse."

"Do you mean the politics?"

"Politics, the elections, the government, and the people too," she said. "Here's a prime minister who's been assassinated and what do people do? They elect the man who practically incited the assassins."

There was nothing new about that. I could have told her so.

"Yes, but there's the suicide bombing," I interrupted, more out of disappointment than from my assigned role. "Sometimes people have to make hard decisions. Whatever Netanyahu did to incite right-wing extremists, when the elections came people believed that he was the one who was strong enough to deal with the suicide bombing."

"Yes I understand. There's no denying it," she replied impatiently which meant that back in Israel she must have heard this explanation many times. "But what I'm talking about is that people are frightened to confront the possibility that there might be more than one individual nutter who planned and carried it out."

"You mean the assassination of Rabin?" It was difficult to believe that this was all she had wanted to tell me. "Now, come on, you don't believe that Netanyahu or anybody else at the top had anything to do with it."

"I'm not saying that Netanyahu planned it," she interrupted impatiently. "What really worried me, what I found so scary is that people don't want to know how many nutters were involved, how many there are in the country. The country is full of them, I tell you, and they don't want to know. How can they expect to make peace while we have so many nutters?"

I couldn't think of a thing to say. I wasn't convinced she was right but didn't want to contradict her any further. Besides, her impatient tone indicated that I no longer needed to play my agreed role, to defend her people when she was attacking them, for she wasn't attacking them, she was only worried for them.

My silence helped her calm down and get to what she'd actually meant to tell me from the beginning.

"Anyway, what I wanted to say is that though I was worried, even frightened by what I'd seen and heard, I didn't feel the way I used to when I went to Israel. I mean before we were together. There were things in the past that would have made me angry or sick, but not now."

She looked at me, probably expecting me to be appreciative or at least curious. "I no longer hated Israel and questioned why I had come back, which is what I'd done in the past."

"Why's that?" I wanted to prove to her that I was really interested but my mind was really elsewhere.

"Because I felt confident," she said, "I no longer felt that the only thing to do is to run away. Our life together has made me feel that there's an alternative."

"How do you mean?"

"I thought about it all while I was alone in one of those small, old-fashioned cafés which I love so much about Tel Aviv. I thought in Israel we grew up to believe that this is our lot, we are a part of it and we have no other choice. We are surrounded by our enemies and the only way to continue existing is to defend what we have and what we are. And in a sense that felt true. But by living with you I realised there's an alternative. I'm living an alternative way of life and so are many people like me, Israelis and Jews who are living outside the borders of their country."

I was amused that she had taken our shared life as a model for an alternative. She seemed to forget that she'd gone to Israel, among other reasons, to escape the boredom of our life together. I wanted to remind her that no matter how proud she was of us being together it was not totally secure. "Yes, but are we a safe alternative?" I asked.

"We were told that there's no alternative because there is no such thing as a safe world," she replied, "but there is, or could be."

"How can you be so sure?"

"You, because of you," she said looking at me. "Supposedly you belong to the other side, to the enemy, but you want a different life. I don't mean a different life in terms of a utopia, but only a simple alternative. By definition this is what most ordinary people want, no?"

I agreed but I wasn't sure. "But aren't you relying too much on the good intentions of the so-called ordinary people?"

"It's not a matter of good intentions it's more of adjusting their thinking to their nature."

Again I nodded, but I was uncertain. I just didn't want to contradict her. She sounded so sure, and more importantly, happy that I didn't want to spoil things for her. Besides, I wanted her to finish what she had to say so I could tell her all about my script.

"Yes, you're right," I said, "however the problem is how to make people think according to their nature?" and without waiting for her response I went on, "funnily enough this is one issue which my script deals with."

"Really? How amusing!"

"Yes, well it's about a young man who fails to know what his life is about until it's too late." I was pleased that we managed to move on so smoothly to my script and went on telling her all about it.

She seemed happy, and I was happy.

That evening we made love in a completely fulfilling way, something we had achieved on very few occasions. We were so satisfied that it was as if we were reliving those days after we had overcome our awkward beginning, and certainly before sex became infrequent and dull. We had regained a lost sensation.

Ruth smoked a cigarette. I hadn't seen her smoking since we first met at that party.

"Most people I know in Israel smoke," she said.

"Did you smoke there?"

"Sometimes, in the evening" she said and added sarcastically, "when the argument got heated."

"Did you have arguments?" I asked and added after a moment of hesitation, "with your eldest sister?"

"With her and with everybody else," she replied overlooking the implication in my question.

"Did she ask you how you could sleep with an Arab?"

"Who? You mean Edith?" She didn't sound too keen to mention her, "I didn't see her that often."

"What else did you do apart from smoking and arguing?" I teased.

"How do you mean?" She sounded a bit annoyed.

"Did you meet any of your old boyfriends?"

"Oh, Ibrahim, for God's sake!"

"I'm just joking!"

Then we were silent. But I couldn't remain silent for long. I wanted to provoke her.

"Tell me a secret, a really interesting secret," I said.

"Really?" she asked. She was amused and surprised by my request. "What about?"

"You, your life, your visit to Israel." I was hoping that she'd tell me she'd met an ex-boyfriend, that he'd made a pass at her and she had been tempted. That she wanted to see what it was like to sleep again with someone she'd slept with more than twenty years earlier.

"Well, there was something I've wanted to tell you a long time ago," she said.

I felt slightly let down that it wasn't going to be something from her trip.

"Something I ought to have told you, that you ought to be aware of."

I was expecting her to reveal a dreadful secret.

"You know the land our house is built on, well, it belonged to an Arab."

She waited for my reaction but I didn't know what to say. I was dissatisfied. I was hoping to hear something personal, something personally unexpected, not about politics, but about her. But no, here she was telling me about land which belonged to an Arab.

"What's so secret about that?" I replied, irritated. "Isn't that the case with most Israeli homes and properties?"

"No! Many Israelis refused to take land that belonged to Arabs." she said. "Anyway what I want to say, too, is that when I was a child and wanted to upset my parents I used to say to them 'what shall we do if the owner of the land comes back?'"

I tried to sound approving but I couldn't. "What did they say?" I asked without great enthusiasm.

"What do you expect? 'Shut up!'"

"Yes, that's what parents are good at." I wanted to trivialise what she was saying so we could return to personal matters. I very much wanted her to tell me about a boyfriend back in Israel. But she didn't and we were silent for a while.

"Now I could tell you a secret," I said and told her how I'd felt when she'd gone and how I tried to sleep with Nada.

"Did you really?" she looked at me coldly and then left the bed.

"Where are you going?" I asked and realised I had been stupid to tell her about Nada.

She got dressed. "I'm going to stay with Yael," she said

without looking at me. She must've had tears in her eyes and didn't want me to see.

"What? Why?"

"Nothing, I'm just going to stay the night with my friend." She dressed, picked up her bag, and left the flat.

She left but I knew she'd come back. She was incapable of leaving, I said to myself. Besides, we had become like a married couple.

11

First Netanyahu talked about "peace with security", then Ruth came back, then she suggested that we should go to Israel together.

After staying with Yael for only a few days, she came back, saying that she'd overreacted, that obviously I hadn't been serious about having an affair with Nada otherwise I wouldn't have told her.

"We must forget it," she said.

I was relieved but also curious to know why she was so forgiving and wondered whether she meant it. However, her coming back so quickly was not totally unexpected, I'd known that she would. She'd got used to our living together and she couldn't simply leave for good. I could just imagine her sitting in Yael's flat, suffering a constant sense of estrangement, a sense which would become totally stifling – for if she'd really thought of leaving me for good, she would have had to start looking for a place to live. She couldn't stay with her friend forever and would have had to find a place of her own and then, what was more frightening, remain alone. Knowing Ruth very well, the idea of house-hunting would be troubling enough and the thought of having to move alone into a new flat in an unfamiliar area would certainly make her deeply depressed.

Her tight financial situation wouldn't make it any easier.

She couldn't simply rent a place where she would feel reasonably comfortable and secure. The best she could afford would be a simple studio flat in a poor residential area.

So she came back. I expected her to open the subject of my attempt to have an affair with Nada. I didn't believe that she wanted to forget it completely. I actually wanted to talk about it so we could discuss our whole relationship. But Ruth wasn't in the mood to be serious. She kept telling me jokes, jokes which she'd heard from Yael. When she had finished tidying up, she started cooking dinner. I offered to help but she refused.

"Ibrahim, sweetheart, I'll be an Arab woman tonight."

I knew that she was only teasing me.

"Good! But as long as you don't become like Aunt Souad," I replied.

"Why?"

"Because her husband has to do everything. Cleaning, cooking, baking, you name it."

"Really? And what does she do?"

"Nothing, apart from smoking shisha and visiting relatives and neighbours."

"Does he love her so much?"

"Yes, he loves her, but it isn't love that makes him do everything for her. It's fear of her big mouth."

She laughed.

"Shall I open a bottle of wine?" I asked.

She nodded. She was still smiling. Standing by the kitchen table, opening the wine, while looking at her, I was amused to see her in such a good mood, laughing and making funny remarks. For a moment I wondered if she was drunk.

"Is that a new skirt? I haven't seen you wearing it before."

"No, it's not new." She seemed pleased that I had noticed what she was wearing, something which I rarely did. But, then again, Ruth herself was not into shopping and flashy clothes.

"It's Yael's actually. Well, she gave it to me."

"Gave it to you?"

"Yes! I tried it and she thought that it suited me more than it suited her. So she gave it to me."

"Is that because you are used to long skirts?"

"No! Yael likes long skirts too." She again looked amused because I was showing an interest.

"Don't you like me wearing long skirts?"

"I don't mind," I said, "I just wondered why you always wear long skirts and dresses."

"Because I have deformed legs," she laughed. "I don't know. I've always liked wearing long clothes even when the weather is hot."

"You like to hide, to hide yourself," I said.

"I like to hide," she replied, "and so do you."

Later that evening, while we were in the sitting room, enjoying the peace that we had re-established after weeks of separation and tension, she returned to her recent visit to Israel. Beginning where she had left off, before I told her about Nada and we had that fight, she recalled the lovely times she had with her sister Dalya.

"We went together to all the places that I like in Tel

Aviv," she said. "Dalya was good. She would sneak out of work just to go around with me."

She loved Dalya and talked about her with great affection. And as if to please her I told her that I would love to meet her sister.

"You would really like her," she said, happy that we were talking about Dalya.

"Why don't you ask her to come here?" I asked.

"To London?" Surprised, she sounded as if such a thing had never crossed her mind.

"Yes, she could stay with us for a couple of weeks," I said.

"No, Dalya wouldn't like it here," she said dreamily as if recalling the image of her sister. "Dalya wouldn't like to be anywhere but in Tel Aviv. I have a better idea," she said after a while. "Why don't *we* go to Israel?"

"Yes, why not?" I said adding jokingly, "I could also claim my right of return."

"No, I mean it," she said. "It would be nice. You would meet Dalya and Rafi and we could see the country together."

"Are you serious?" I asked but I knew she was. That's why I talked about claiming the right of return. Ruth knew that I didn't believe in such a right, that I was only trying to turn her idea into a joke.

This wasn't the first time she'd suggested that we go to Israel together but she'd usually been joking.

"When we get fed up with London we could go to Israel," she would say. "You could demand your right of return and become an Israeli citizen!"

"Yes, and you'd be glorified as an Arab lover!" I would reply and we would both laugh.

But now she was serious. Obviously her visit to Israel had encouraged her to consider the real possibility of going there together.

"You could visit the village your parents came from and we could stay in Acre for a couple of days."

"You must be joking!" I was worried that she might insist on this idea. I was worried too that I would weaken and go along with her plan.

"It would be a great experience for you," she said. "You might come back with an idea for a film."

"I already have an idea for a film," I said, reminding her of my recent script. I was annoyed that she appeared to have forgotten all about it.

"Yes I know, but I mean an idea for a documentary. Just think, a documentary about going to see your parents' village. People at Channel 4 would kill themselves for it."

Shaking my head, I recalled my earlier efforts to contact TV producers, "I'm not sure that anybody would care, let alone kill themselves, for an idea of mine." But the main reason I didn't want to go to Israel was because I was still frightened of the Israelis. I didn't know how to tell Ruth. I didn't have the courage to say: Look I grew up thinking of Israelis as our enemies and fearing them. I've had no firsthand knowledge of Israeli society and I've always seen Israelis as soldiers and ruthless fighters. Living with you and meeting friendly Israelis has not helped me overcome such a deeply rooted fear. Somehow, you and other Israelis I've known in London, do not seem like proper Israelis, and certainly not like those I saw or heard of in Lebanon. Living outside Israel, you, and they, are critical of your country and somehow are stripped of the scary power of those who are there; you are here, in London, and no more frightening than anybody else.

No, I couldn't say this to Ruth. I didn't want to spoil the evening.

"You'd love it there," she said, persisting.

"I would probably be arrested at the airport," I replied.

"Why? You have a British passport?"

"Yes I do, but my name is Ibrahim Al-Asmar, born in Lebanon."

"So what? In Lebanon you were only a student and a film-maker."

"Yes, a film-maker who worked for the PLO! They'd love that."

"Oh, come on!" she exclaimed impatiently. "Things have changed. Lots of the PLO go to Israel now, even those who were once terrorists."

"Terrorists?"

"I mean *fedayeen*!" she snapped, "don't start picking on every word I say!"

She was embarrassed that she'd called Palestinian fighters terrorists, or so I thought, and wanted to hide her embarrassment by hitting out. I remained silent. I didn't want to spoil the peaceful time we were having. She didn't want to spoil it either. Rather than sulking, her usual response when challenged, she remained calmly silent.

We sat there sipping red wine

"Do you want to go to bed?" she asked after a while.

And so we did and just as we started making love, the thought of going to Israel burst into my mind like a cold wind gusting through a door, I couldn't continue.

"What's wrong?" Her voice was sympathetic, which made me feel embarrassed. "Don't you fancy me any more?" she asked straightforwardly.

"What?" I was surprised. I didn't expect her to ask such a question. "I don't fancy the idea of going to Israel."

"Fine!" she replied, irritated. "Stop thinking about it now!"

After that we said no more; we gradually drifted off to sleep. I slept deeply and had a dream, a nightmare actually, one which I'd never managed to forget.

First I saw the face of Cousin Maryam, which became the face of Ruth. I dreamt that Ruth and I were in Jerusalem. We were wandering through the narrow winding Arab market. Ruth was busy examining what was for sale, mostly kitsch tourist souvenirs. But there were also a few unusual pieces which Ruth, with the experienced eye of a local, pointed out. Sellers tried to draw her attention elsewhere but when she responded in Hebrew this was enough to deter them from their patter. Talking in Hebrew seemed a powerful enough sign to convince sellers to refrain from trying to sell her kitsch. Others, however, were not so deterred and talked in Hebrew too.

I myself was not interested in all that but I was amused to see Palestinians as salesmen flattering their customers with whatever language or words they knew; Hebrew,

English and even Yiddish. This was the first time that I had seen any of my people acting as sweet-talking salesmen. Back in Lebanon, Palestinian shopkeepers never tried to do such a thing. They considered flattery and haggling a form of begging and at best an attempt to cheat people. It was deemed shameful; only godless city merchants did this kind of thing.

Ruth and I continued to wander through the long market until we reached what seemed the end of the tourist area and the beginning of a residential neighbourhood.

"We must go back now!" Ruth warned in what sounded unmistakably like a warning.

"Don't be frightened, you're with me," I said, jokingly, and wanted to carry on walking but she seized me by the arm. "Don't go there, please!" she implored. I saw a look of fear on her face (it was the same look which I had seen two days ago, before she left – but I'll come to that). It was so telling a look that it almost frightened me too. I turned and started walking back. But, no what am I doing? I asked myself, stopping suddenly.

"No, damn you!" I shouted at her, "You can be as frightened as you like but I don't have to be."

"Please, let's go back!" she begged me again, but I ignored her and continued into the Arab residential area.

"People here are ok," she said following me, trying to explain that her fear did not spring from prejudice, "but you can't tell whether terrorists are hiding here."

"Terrorists" I yelled, and if only to defy her, I kept on walking.

"Look, whatever you call them," she implored, "they're dangerous!"

"Yes, and so are your soldiers!" I shouted and stopped to see the effect of what I'd just said. The next thing I remember was that a group of masked men surrounded us, waving their pistols in our faces and ordering us to walk on in front of them.

They spoke a mixture of Arabic, Hebrew and English. I wanted to protest that they had made a mistake but looking at them I realised all I would get back in return was a kick or a blow from a pistol butt.

We were pushed through narrow alleys and eventually down steps into what looked like a cellar. We were locked in. It was dark and again the face of Cousin Maryam appeared.

"Whatever you want to say to them, don't say it in Hebrew!" I warned Ruth. She, however, was so terrified she looked unable to utter a word.

"It'll be all right!" I said. I was still frightened but I was also confident that it would be enough for me to speak Arabic and prove to them that I was Palestinian. They would realise their mistake and set us free. The important thing was that Ruth must not utter a word of Hebrew otherwise they would shoot us both. They would assume that we were both Israelis and kill us. It certainly wouldn't help me to say I was only her partner or her friend. How could I be the partner of an Israeli woman without being a Mossad agent, in short a traitor myself? They might well interrogate and beat me before eventually shooting me. But what if they gave me no chance to explain? What if they came in and shot us directly? Back in Lebanon I knew of militia men who would capture people on the mere suspicion that they belonged to an enemy group and would shoot them.

No they wouldn't do that, they wouldn't do that, I kept telling myself. And they didn't. After what felt like several hours they came back, accompanied this time by someone whom I assumed to be their leader. I started talking to him in Arabic, explaining that they must have made a mistake. He was startled to hear me speaking Arabic with a mixed Lebanese and Palestinian accent and when I showed him my passport which stated that I was born in Lebanon, he grew angry with his comrades: "Congratulations! You have kidnapped a Palestinian!"

"He could be a collaborator!" one of his comrades suggested.

"Oh, yes? A collaborator all the way from London!"

"What about the woman?" asked the same guy. "She could be an Israeli."

The leader gave him a look which meant "shut up." He was still annoyed by him, but then he turned to me.

"She's Romanian!" I yelled.

Ruth was almost hysterical and incapable of speech, but thankfully she didn't understand what was being said. But then again it wasn't her face that I saw, but Maryam's.

"Is she your wife?" he asked.

I didn't know how to answer this question. I was worried they might be religious and if I said "no" they would certainly not approve. And if I said she was my wife I might be asked to prove it.

I was also worried that they might ask for Ruth's passport. She didn't have it with her as she didn't feel the need to carry any identification.

"She's my fiancée." I said, "We intend to get married when we get back to London. We want to get married and go to Lebanon to visit my family."

The leader looked particularly impressed by this last lie. Here it was, he must have thought, a good Palestinian who's taking his bride to his family for their blessing. He looked happy and didn't want to detain us any longer, "Congratulations in advance! And I'm sorry about all this! You can leave now," he said and we were rushed out.

We walked hurriedly and if it hadn't been for the fear of arousing their suspicions again we would have run. However before we managed to get far I thought of going back. I actually turned and went back. I wanted to confess to the leader of the group that she was actually Israeli.

When I woke up the following morning I felt terrible. The images were frighteningly vivid but I was stunned by my intention to turn Ruth in, to betray her. It was as if I had given in to a desire which I had subconsciously wished for a long time.

That day, and for the following three or four days, that dream and particularly its ending, overwhelmed me. Why did I have it? Did it mean that I was so eager to get rid of Ruth, or was it only because I wanted to see Israelis punished?

I thought of telling her. I thought if I tell her I could simply turn the whole disturbing thing into a joke and relieve myself of my torment. But I was still worried that she might be hurt. She was bound to think the dream was an expression of my hidden desire that I wanted her out of my life. But dreams don't mean what they seem to, I could argue. She wouldn't agree. I was going to betray her, and it really felt so terrible that for the whole of that day I couldn't look at her without feeling ashamed of myself. Then I remembered the images of Cousin Maryam's face.

Yes, relieved, I saw it several times. It must mean something, I thought knowing very well that I was only trying to free myself from the tormenting sense of shame. This dream wasn't about Ruth – it was about Cousin Maryam, Maryam the victim, the one who had been killed but whom everybody claimed had just disappeared. It was the story of Maryam, I said to myself, returning in a dream about recent events involving Ruth and me.

Better still, I went further to absolve myself of guilt, it was an old nightmare taking on a new form. It was the same dream that I used to have back in Lebanon, the same one in which I saw Cousin Maryam and Uncle Ahmad surrounded by an angry mob.

This is what I said to myself, but I wasn't convinced.

Part Three

12

First everybody said that the peace process was over, then my father died.

My father died all of a sudden. Uncle Khalil phoned me to tell me the sad news. I was as surprised to hear Uncle Khalil's voice as to hear the news of my father's death. I hadn't seen or heard from him since the spring of 1982, almost two months before the Israeli invasion of Lebanon. I was living in Beirut then but had gone to El-Bass, our camp, to visit my parents. My mother begged me to go and visit my uncles, Mohammad and Khalil, "Your father rarely goes there and they feel neglected," she said, "especially your uncle Khalil. After what has happened to them, if you know what I mean."

I nodded quickly to spare her the embarrassment of an explanation. Mother was referring to what had happened to Cousin Maryam. She was the daughter of Uncle Khalil and though she'd disappeared nearly eight years earlier (or so we believed, or at least claimed to believe) her parents never recovered. When Uncle Khalil phoned to tell me that my father had passed away, when again I heard that resigned tone of voice of his, the pain was all the greater because I was reminded of the time of Maryam's misfortune. Uncle Khalil and Aunt Aisha, his wife, were shattered. There was nothing more heart-breaking than to see this peaceful couple in such a state.

Now my father was dead and this would only bring back distressing memories and cause more sadness for Uncle Khalil and his wife. On the telephone he tried to sound as consoling as possible yet I felt that he was more in need of consolation than me.

"Keep faith!" he said in his resigned tone of voice.

"I will!" I whispered and nearly burst into tears.

When I put the receiver down Ruth came out of the study where she had been working on a translation of an essay for a newspaper. I told her the news and she was as shocked as I was. She cried but then, as if she realised it would be more appropriate to be supportive than to sit by me crying, she asked, "Do you want me to get in touch with the travel agent I usually deal with, or do you know someone better?"

I didn't reply. I just sat there, motionless and silent, trying to absorb the awful news. He's dead, I said to myself as if trying to make myself believe it. I didn't expect him to die just then. He was hardly sixty-five years old. I knew that he'd been ill, but I was told that it wasn't terminal. It was just the result of a simple accident; he had fallen off a ladder and fractured his leg. "He's being well-treated," my brother told me, "don't worry!"

Two weeks later he was dead.

In hospital he'd been angry and depressed and couldn't stand being bed-bound. He had worked from the age of nine, and he couldn't stop working. Not that he particularly enjoyed work or was good at what he did, but it seemed as if work was the only proof that he was alive. As far back as I could remember, he woke up every day at five o'clock and went out. He was a simple workman; he worked as a farmer and builder and did anything that didn't require him to be more than a worker. Even when he had no work, he would get up at dawn and go out. Wrapped in his coat, woolly hat and scarf, he would go to the seaside. He had been brought up in a coastal village and loved the sea; he sought and found solace on its shores. He would walk along the sand for hours on end, looking around, and examining curious objects that had been abandoned by night waves. Bringing such objects back from his long walks was important to him and gave him the rewarding sense that he was still working and had earned something. He would select whatever he hoped might be of use to us or our relatives and friends. Unlike parents of most of my friends he was not interested in collecting and keeping things for himself.

So when he became bed-bound he grew irritated and depressed and then died.

I was sad of course. My sadness, however, was not the natural sadness of a son grieving for his dead father. I didn't love him enough to grieve for him naturally. I wasn't close to him. On the contrary, I often felt as if he were a stranger to us — an intruder in our lives, my mother's, my brothers', my sisters' and mine. He seemed to me like someone who had accidentally come into our lives, and having faced no resistance or protest, he remained there but without pleasure or a sense of triumph. He was simply there. Sometimes I felt that the only reason he remained with us was because he couldn't find a better, a more interesting or more comfortable, place. As I remember it now, it is as though both he and we were caught up in a fateful situation which we accepted, reluctantly.

My father was a lonely and mostly a silent man. He didn't seem to believe in language as an essential medium of communication unless it was used as a tool of abuse. What made him worse was that he was easily irritated and provoked. I think he felt stifled in our company, and not only our company but any human company. He'd only a few friends, two or three at the most, and they were all like him, silent.

Of course he was never oblivious to the fact that he was a husband and father of five children but that only made him more depressed. He must have felt that he was tricked into getting married and becoming a father of so many children. Though in our society married people often had seven or eight, sometimes nine or ten children, for my father having us was an unforgivable mistake.

"If it wasn't for them, I would have fled. I would have gone, disappeared," he would say, bitterly, pointing at us, his children.

Fleeing and disappearing. Yes, that was exactly what father wished to do. Where he would flee to, he never mentioned, nor did I believe that he knew. The idea was to disappear, to be somewhere he couldn't be recognised. And perhaps his repeatedly expressed desire to disappear made me regard him as a stranger who reluctantly entered our lives. It was a thought which remained with me all those years, even when I heard of his illness and death.

But it wasn't only from us his children he wanted to run

away. From his parents, his brothers and sisters too. When he got married my grandfather offered to buy him a piece of land on which to build a house for him and his wife. But my father refused. It was just next to where my grandparents, Uncle Mohammad and Uncle Khalil lived. But he didn't want to be close to them all. He actually wanted to get as far away from them as possible. My grandfather used to call him the stepson, "Where is my stepson?" he would ask when there was a family gathering and my father was late to turn up or, as often happened, didn't turn up at all. Unsurprisingly my father didn't mind being called a stepson. He wanted to be detached from his family and wanted them to accept his detachment as a matter of fact.

Recalling him now, after more than twenty years, he seemed like someone who profoundly believed that he was an orphan. His fondness for being alone, traversing the desolate seashore, was only one aspect of being this lonely child of nature.

After my grandfather died my father rarely visited his brothers and sisters, and if he did he said little. Nor did the rest of the family expect him to say much. He didn't want to get involved in their affairs — not even after the tragedy of Cousin Maryam when every member of the family saw it as their duty to be together. He wished to leave them, to leave the camp and the whole of Lebanon, to go to another country. In all the time I knew him I never heard him praising any of his brothers and sisters apart from Uncle Karim and Aunt Nadia and they both lived abroad, Uncle Karim in Germany and Aunt Nadia with her husband in Saudi Arabia.

Thinking about him now, I realise that his desire to flee, even his assiduous commitment to work was an attempt to avoid socialising and ultimately to shut himself away from the rest of the world. After my brother Fadi died he managed to do just that. He even tried to encourage us to do the same. He bought us a television set; our home was the first in the street to possess one. He thought that by providing us with a source of entertainment we would dispense with the company of others: friends, relatives and neighbours. And he almost succeeded, instead of going out to see our friends and relatives we spent all our free time watching television. The problem was that even more people started visiting us – those of our age wanted to be our friends just so they could watch television. There came a time when the terrace in front of our house looked like an open-air cinema. My father cursed the moment he bought the set but nevertheless he had to play the role of hospitable host, nodding and smiling at the visiting audience.

The more I thought about him, the sadder I grew. I saw him as a man who had lived his life entrapped by circumstances which mostly were not of his own doing or choosing. Worse still, he was living by values and traditions which were no longer fit for such circumstances.

From the age of fourteen until he died, my father lived as a refugee. This was visibly imprinted on his life though he tried to ignore it. He lived most of his life in a refugee camp, relying for his survival, and later for ours, on doing odd jobs and on regular aid from UNRWA. Despite this, like other Palestinians of his generation who had been compelled to escape to Lebanon from their villages in northern Palestine, he behaved as if he were still living in his own country. In his conviction and manner he conducted himself as a landowner or farmer for whom seeking work was not an issue. And just like a farmer, or the farmer he would have been back in Palestine, he married at the early age of eighteen and by thirty he was the father of five children.

It was expected of him to be a proud family man, and at the beginning he was, or pretended to be. Soon, however, he realised that he'd made a big mistake, that he'd failed to take into consideration the fact that he was simply a refugee, and that he should have planned his life accordingly. He must also have known that he lacked the courage to come to terms with the hard truth that he was without a homeland, without the security of owning land and without a permanent job.

My father had no illusion that Palestinians would ever go back. People around him believed, especially in the optimistic time of the rise of Gamal Abdel Nasser, that liberating Palestine was inevitable. He, on the other, despaired too soon.

"Palestine's gone," I heard him saying frequently, shaking his head in despair, "it's been lost forever!"

Neither Nasser nor, later, the emergence of the fedayeen movement made any difference to his convictions.

After the Arab defeat in 1967, a new generation of Palestinians, born and brought up in camps, became politically active and joined the fedayeen. But that didn't give him the slightest hope of returning to his land, indeed he laughed at the fedayeen, "Those fools think they are going to liberate Palestine, do they? What nonsense!"

When my eldest brother Fadi joined The Democratic Front, one of the fedayeen organizations, he went mad.

"What! Do you want to be a loser?" he screamed. "Instead of studying and getting a qualification for a good career you join those buggers!"

Fadi tried to ignore him but that only made Father angrier. He went for him, hitting him, "Do you want to have a miserable life like me?"

"No, I don't want to be a loser," Fadi yelled back defiantly. "I don't want to be like you!" He pushed Father back firmly, causing him to stagger and almost fall to the floor.

Father was shocked. He had never expected a son of his, no matter how grown up, to answer him back, let alone push him. He was silent as if he had lost the capacity to speak.

"No I don't want to become a loser like you and others like you," Fadi went on, probably encouraged by my father's silence, "that's why I have joined the fedayeen. They're not losers like you. They're trying to get back what people like you have lost and didn't even have the courage to fight for. Fucking cowards!"

Until that moment he made sense, but then he started speaking like an orator shouting about fighting Zionism and Imperialism and the backward Arab forces who were the main enemy of the revolution. We didn't know whether to be more shocked by him pushing Father or by his sudden use of such rhetoric. This rhetoric was not new to us; leaders and organisers of the fedayeen used it all the time and people like us accepted it as a tool of their trade. Such hollow words did not correspond to the reality of our everyday life and meant nothing to us, and to hear them coming out of the mouth of my brother sounded so strange, so ridiculous.

And it was because he talked in that way that my father managed to recover quickly. He exclaimed contemptuously, "Since you are such a hero then get out of my house! Get out now! Go to your hero friends and liberate Palestine!"

"Yes, we will!" Fadi shouted furiously and left.

That was the last time we saw him. A few weeks later he was killed during a clash between two fedayeen factions. We were heart-broken; most of all, my father. He felt responsible for Fadi's death. Not because he had thrown him out. We all knew that my brother was killed accidentally, and that he could have been killed no matter what my father had done. In those days clashes between different factions were a familiar danger in the camp; many people were accidentally killed. No, my father felt responsible because he made the mistake of behaving as if he was still living in Palestine. He had made the mistake of bringing up children in conditions where children could be killed so accidentally, so simply.

"People like us should never have children," he cried out bitterly, "what for? To see them being killed for nothing."

He never forgave himself. He grieved for my brother

more than any of us. I believe that he grieved for the rest of his life. And though he stopped expressing the desire to be out of it all, one could feel that then, more than ever, he would have liked to be so. Although I was sad to know of his death, I couldn't help thinking that perhaps at last his wish had come true. Perhaps he always wanted to die.

I was sad but didn't cry. I didn't want to grieve. Ruth cried and grieved. She remembered her own father and cried and relived her own sorrow all over again. She wept, yet she felt that it was her duty to pull herself together and help me to get ready to go to Lebanon.

"Do you think you can get a flight soon enough to attend the funeral?" she asked, picking up the phone to find out about flights to Beirut.

"I'm not going," I said in a tone of deliberate calmness.

"What? Are you serious?"

"Yes, I'm serious," I replied in the same calm way.

"Why? Don't you want to be at your father's funeral? Don't you want to be with your family at such a time? They need you and you need to be with them."

I looked at her and to my surprise she looked as if she'd known that I had no intention of going. And although she might have felt I was right in my decision, she also knew that she should encourage me to go.

But no, she didn't think I was right. She'd expected my response because she thought that perhaps I was feeling guilty and to overcome my guilt I was refusing to believe that my father had died.

"Denial is no way to avoid grief," she said, trying to be both honest and sympathetic.

"Denial? Who's in denial?" I asked, irritated both by her accusation and her use of this sort of terminology. "I'm not in denial. I know he's dead. His life's finished and I don't need to go all the way there to believe it. It's not worth it."

"Not worth it. Attending your father's funeral is not worth it? If it were my father I would have gone to Israel like a shot!"

"Yes, I know," I replied and added coldly and heartlessly, "there's nothing you would like to do more than to grieve for your father. Or just simply grieve!"

"How could you say that?"

"I'm sorry," and I was sorry, but I was also impatient with her. "Look, my father wasn't like yours. Yours was a good man, an achiever, mine was just a self-pitying loser!"

"What?" she screamed. "How could you say such a thing when he's just died?"

"Because that's what he was, a self-pitying loser! No point in denying it and I'm not going all the way back for the sake of his funeral."

"I didn't believe you could be such a heartless bastard!" She rushed into the bedroom.

That night I went out and got drunk.

13

First there were more suicide bombings then she stopped sleeping with me.

For a whole week after the news of my father's death we slept separately, Ruth in the bedroom and I on the sofa in the sitting room. She couldn't forgive me for not going to my father's funeral.

"I can't stand being close to you," she said, and cried.

Of course she wasn't crying about my father. She didn't know him. I'd hardly told her anything about him; I'd hardly told her anything about any of my family. No, she was crying about her own father; she was reliving her own grief. But she was angry with me too. There she was crying her eyes out for her father who had died some thirty years earlier while I, who had just lost mine, could not mourn.

I tried to explain to her that I wasn't as close to my father as she'd been to hers, indeed I was anything but close, but even if I had been I would not have mourned as deeply as her.

"You lost your father when you were only eleven," I went on trying to win her sympathy. "Yours was an early loss and it's understandable that you have never got over it. I'm no longer young; no longer new to the sense of loss. What I've seen, what I've been through, has made me less vulnerable."

But she just sat on the sofa, motionless, staring fixedly at the blank television screen.

"Had you lost your father at the age you are now, you probably wouldn't grieve for as long." I was becoming slightly irritated by her lack of response. "The more we suffer loss, the less we grieve."

She didn't seem to agree. As a matter of fact she looked as if she didn't even want to listen to me, that after what I'd done, I wasn't worth listening to. She gave me a look as if to say that at last I'd revealed my real self, the cowardice and indifference of which I was made.

I wanted to dispel the tension between us and when talking didn't work I suggested we go to the theatre or to a restaurant; we hadn't been out for a long time. But that didn't work either, it only made her angrier.

"Your father has just been buried and you want to go out enjoying yourself?"

I tried to explain that I didn't just want to enjoy myself but rather to clear the air. "How about inviting a couple of friends, or visiting Yael?" I suggested but she only gave me that look which was meant to say that she'd given up on me.

She remained sad and angry and didn't calm down until days later when I nearly broke my right leg. I was trying to hang a picture which I had first promised to do when she bought it some weeks earlier, but due to my customary resistance, I hadn't. I tried to do it now because she was angry and I wanted to make it up to her.

For days I had been fixing things which for a long time she'd been telling me needed to be done. But neither changing a light bulb nor fixing the door of the kitchen cupboard was sufficient to get her out of her unhappiness until I fell off the stepladder.

She rushed up to me, extremely worried, "Shall I call an ambulance?"

"No!" I replied firmly, in spite of the sharp sudden pain, "nothing's broken." I got up slowly, and with some effort walked to the sofa, trying my best not to limp. I was delighted to see her so worried about me.

She didn't think I was all right, "You must go to casualty and get it checked."

"No, I'm all right," I replied with difficulty, trying to conceal my pain. The important thing for me then was that her mood had finally changed.

It was the prolonged state of her mood that I couldn't bear. For me one could become angry, or sad, but only for a short time. After that one must cheer up or, as I used to do, slip quietly into a state of resignation and subtle melancholy. There was no point being angry or sad for a long time. For if my indifference towards my father's death disgusted Ruth, the atmosphere she created frightened me. It created such a tormenting sense of uncertainty in my life that at one point I thought I was prepared to leave her just in order to put an end to it. Uncertainty frightened me, and made me panic and unable to focus on the simplest of things.

Luckily it didn't last. Eventually she opened her heart to me. She told me that she was troubled not so much because the death of my father had reopened the wound of her own grief, but rather because she remembered that when her father was killed they – her mother, sisters, and brother – couldn't mourn him in the way they wanted.

"We were heartbroken," she said. "We were devastated, but everybody else was happy. People were celebrating in the streets. It was a great time of victory; Israel had won the war. How could you mourn when everybody was happy celebrating victory?"

They mourned of course, only it was a public mourning. Her father was decorated a war hero, a dead war hero.

"We owed it to him," said the representatives of the government and the army who took part in the funeral and made public speeches, "the whole country owes it to Nathan and to people like Nathan."

Her father was a war hero and his funeral a public affair. She was supposed to be happy with the victory and proud of her father who had died making it possible. The victory was hers more than anybody else's, they told her.

"But I didn't feel like a victor. I felt defeated. I didn't feel proud of my father, he was gone, he was dead, and worse still we couldn't grieve for him as people do when someone they love dies. His death was a betrayal; treating his death as a public affair robbed us of our right to mourn the way we wanted, privately. We were devastated, but everybody wanted us to be happy and proud. We were all devastated. We never got over it, especially my mother and I."

Her mother was depressed from then until the day she died. She died of grief. Ruth too was depressed, "I suffered from depression for years but I hid it. My mother was in a terrible state and I felt I must try and help her not make things worse. But you know things stay with you and whenever something happens, something that reminds me of my father's death, I relive the whole episode all over again."

"But why are you angry with me?"

"Because you have the opportunity which I didn't have. You have the chance to mourn your father privately, but you turned it down so casually. I can't understand it. You don't know how important it is to have the chance to grieve without some bastard from the government or army watching you and making you feel ashamed of yourself because you don't appreciate the greatness of what your father has done!"

She went on, so overcome by sorrow that she might have been talking to herself. "Every time they saw me crying they would say, 'Your father has sacrificed his life for his country, for you, for all of us!' as if that was enough to make me forget the fact that he was gone, that I could no longer see him and hear his voice again." She wept. "Grief is a private matter and people should be left to grieve privately."

Now I realised that it was the death of her father that was the real cause of her decision to leave Israel. His death created the rift between Ruth and her country, and whatever happened after that only added to the widening of this rift.

I was sure of this because when she was talking I recognised a similar rift in my own life. I remembered how my brother's early death was the beginning of my indifference to politics. "When someone so close to you dies, no matter in what circumstances," I said, remembering Fadi, "it sets you apart from the rest. It creates a rift between you and your people. I know the importance of having the chance to mourn privately. I've experienced it too." I told her about Fadi. "Just like you when your father died, we were heartbroken, especially my father."

And it was because my father was so heartbroken that he insisted on treating Fadi's death for what it really was, a death caused by irresponsible behaviour. He angrily but resolutely refused to turn Fadi's funeral into a public display. Two representatives from the Democratic Front had come to see us and expressed their wish to organise the funeral themselves.

"Fadi must be buried as a martyr," they said, "his death is a loss for the cause!"

My father threw them out. "To hell with you and your whoring cause!" he yelled at them. "My son didn't die a martyr. He didn't die fighting. He was caught in the crossfire between bastards like you!"

"No you mustn't say that!" My uncle Ahmad intervened, "Fadi was a *feday* after all."

Though Uncle Ahmad was very sad, he was a boaster too and he didn't want to waste the opportunity to turn Fadi's funeral into a martyr's funeral. He wanted to become the proud uncle of a martyr.

Encouraged by my uncle's intervention one of the representatives added frantically, "It's true that Comrade Fadi didn't die fighting the Zionist enemy, but his death serves nobody but them and those who killed him are no better than the Zionist enemy. They are practically agents of the Zionist enemy!"

My father couldn't take that. He didn't have the patience to listen to this kind of talk even when he was in a good mood. Now when his own son had been killed for such a stupid reason, when his heart was full of grief and guilt, the last thing he could tolerate was someone blaming it on the so-called Zionist enemy and its agents.

"Out! Get out of my house!" he shouted at the Democratic Front men.

My Uncle Ahmad tried to intervene, at least to calm him down, but he only made my father more enraged. He swiftly turned towards Uncle Ahmad and slapped him, shouting, "You stay out of my business!"

My uncle was shocked; everybody who witnessed the scene was shocked too. Uncle Ahmad was ten years younger than my father, and it wasn't unusual for older brothers to slap younger brothers in a moment of anger. But my father had never done that before. And Uncle Ahmad, himself impetuous and bad tempered, was feared in our street; nobody could mess with our family for fear of Uncle Ahmad. He felt so humiliated that he ran out and stayed away until it was time to carry the coffin to the cemetery. For weeks after that, whenever people mentioned Fadi's funeral they also mentioned how my father slapped Uncle Ahmad in front of everybody.

"The two men from the Democratic Front had to leave," I said to Ruth, concluding my recollection of Fadi's funeral by going back to the original point. "My father didn't want any of them there. This was our affair."

Ruth looked pleased. She looked particularly impressed with my father's attitude.

"I wish we had done the same at my father's funeral."

"Yes, but your father died fighting an enemy," I didn't want her to feel so regretful or, more probably, I didn't want her to feel that my father had behaved bravely while her family hadn't. "Had Fadi died like your father, I mean fighting in a war, my father wouldn't have been able to behave the way he did."

"I think he would," she replied with conviction.

"You think so?" I was amused at how confident she sounded. But she was right, my father would have done the same. He would have resisted turning the funeral of his own son into a public show of heroism. He didn't believe in political parties, and less so in dying for their causes. Ruth knew my father better than me, I said to myself. But that didn't bother me at all. On the contrary, I felt at that moment as close to her as I had ever done.

That night we slept together. We slept in the same bed but we didn't make love.

14

First the Israelis pulled out of Hebron, then they started building a settlement in East Jerusalem, and then the nightmares started again.

Ruth and I had gone back to sleeping together but without making love. Sex became even less of a worry when I started having the same old nightmare which I used to have back in Lebanon, especially in the three years before I left. It was about Cousin Maryam and Uncle Ahmad, and it was understandable that I had it then: I was still in Lebanon and the memory of what had happened to Cousin Maryam had not faded away. But now, after living in London for so many years, I couldn't understand why the nightmare had returned. I just let it happen, the nightmare visiting me night after night.

It all started with the innocent appearance of Cousin Maryam and Uncle Ahmad. They were chatting and smiling when, all of a sudden, a look of terrible fear showed in their faces. Cousin Maryam and Uncle Ahmad stared at an angry mob coming towards them, searching for them, but then passing them by as if they were invisible. At the end of the nightmare, the mob turned on itself, people were stabbed, and there was blood everywhere. Then I woke up.

Night after night I had this same nightmare. Drenched in sweat, I got up and went to the sitting room or the kitchen and sat down until I was calm. Sometimes I made tea or had a glass of whisky before eventually slipping back into bed, quietly. I didn't want Ruth to wake up. I didn't want her to know as I was sure that she would think it was because we had stopped sleeping together. I was worried that that might be true. I remembered the nightmare I'd had when Ruth suggested that we ought to go to Israel together. I had convinced myself it was the same one that was recurring now although in a different form. But what if the nightmare had returned because of Ruth? What if living with Ruth was dragging me back to the dark past? I couldn't tell her because she would cry and blame herself for what was happening to us.

Still she knew. She knew from the first night. She felt my body shivering from what I saw in my dream but she pretended not to notice. She wanted me to tell her in my own time, which I eventually did.

One evening we were sitting in front of the television watching a documentary about sleepwalking. The programme showed that some people could commit a crime while sleepwalking. I couldn't help commenting, jokingly, that I was glad I didn't sleepwalk as well. It was this "as well", which I instantly regretted saying, and which compelled me to tell her about my nightmare.

Contrary to what I had feared, she wasn't upset or worried. She did not, in fact, look in the least surprised. She herself had nightmares whenever she was stressed or unhappy, she said, and started asking questions. She wanted to know details, but she was more curious about Uncle Ahmad and Cousin Maryam.

"What happened to them?"

"To whom?"

"Your uncle and cousin?"

"What? In the dream?"

"No, in real life?"

"They disappeared." I was trying my best to sound as if this was normal, as if I were stating a simple, though strange, fact. I anticipated what was coming and was worried.

"Disappeared?"

"Yes! First Cousin Maryam disappeared and then Uncle Ahmad left!"

"Left?"

"Well, yes …" I hesitated. "I mean he didn't really disappear like Maryam. He left Lebanon and never returned!"

"Where did he go?" Now she sounded more concerned than curious.

"Well, that's it, nobody knows and that's why we came to believe that he had disappeared too."

"When did this happen?"

"Oh, a long time ago," I said. "Twenty years ago, perhaps longer."

"What about her?" she asked suspiciously.

"She's the one who really disappeared … vanished," I was getting impatient. "We looked for her everywhere, but nothing …"

"But how could someone like that disappear?" she asked with growing suspicion. "How old was she?"

"She was only sixteen."

"And she just disappeared?"

"Yes! She went to stay with a family friend in Beirut but she didn't get there and didn't come back. At first we thought she had been kidnapped – there had been many kidnappings at the beginning of the trouble in Lebanon. But no when the driver who had given them a lift returned – he was one of Uncle Khalil's neighbours – he said he had delivered them to the doorstep of the family where Maryam was to stay."

"Them?" Ruth interrupted.

"Yes, she was with Uncle Ahmad. Her family wouldn't let her go to Beirut on her own. He went with her."

"And did he say anything when he came back? Your uncle?"

"He didn't come back. He stayed in Beirut for a few days then left the country."

"Just like that?" she was scornful.

"Well he had been planning to leave anyway. He'd got his papers ready to travel. He wanted to join Uncle Karim in Germany. Many Palestinians went to Germany then. We thought that he'd gone to Germany but Uncle Karim said that he never arrived and we never heard from him again."

I paused, expecting her to ask another question, but she remained silent. Clearly she wasn't convinced. Nor did I expect her to be convinced. It was not a convincing story but we, my family and I, had long come to accept it as I'd just told it. Now that I'd told Ruth I wanted her to accept it too. I decided to tell her the rest. I knew that she didn't want to hear any more but I felt I had to bring the story to a convincing conclusion.

"We weren't as worried about Uncle Ahmad as we were

about Maryam. We looked for her everywhere. We asked relatives, neighbours, friends, but nobody knew anything. Her mother was devastated, the whole family was, too."

"But ..." Ruth started to speak then stopped, a look of deep suspicion on her face.

We both remained silent. I was relieved but as I stood up to leave I heard her say, "She was killed, wasn't she?"

"What?" I was completely taken aback, not by her conclusion but by the speed with which she came to it and by her bluntness.

I was furious, reproaching myself for talking about Cousin Maryam and Uncle Ahmad and about my recurring nightmare. The earth was being dug up, the family secret was being exhumed. How could she have guessed it? No, that wasn't very difficult. The story I told, particularly the clumsy way in which I told it, was bound to lead to such a conclusion. But how dare she, what business was it of hers to guess what, for those involved, should never at any cost be guessed? This was not to be spoken of unless it was absolutely necessary and then only by the family and in a way that would make further curiosity seem an intolerable intrusion. But, let's face it, I'd blown it, I'd been so careless not so much because I was too trusting of Ruth but rather because I had become too far removed from my family to care about their secrets.

"Wasn't she?" tears were running down her face.

"What are you talking about?" I pretended to be shocked at hearing her even suggest such a thing. "Why would she have been killed? What do you know about it anyway? Or are you just letting your imagination run wild?"

"It was one of those honour-killings, wasn't it?"

Close, but not close enough – it wasn't what people here tend to assume.

"What are you talking about?" I replied dismissively, "every time you hear something you analyse it with your own standards and misconceptions."

"My standards and misconceptions?" she asked bitterly, "Or do you mean *ours*?"

"Well ..." I hesitated, "the standards and concepts you were taught!"

"You really don't understand me, do you?" she was disappointed with me.

"Yes I do," I replied angrily. "Every time an Arab woman is mentioned it has to be in connection with her oppression or sexual mutilation or honour-killing."

"Is that how you hear me talk?"

"I don't care how you talk." Fury was blinding me. "Just shut up!"

We had been together for five years and this was the first time I'd shouted at her. It was also the first time that I had told her to shut up and my unexpected reaction made me even more furious. I was worried that I might say something worse so I left the flat.

It was dark but I didn't care. After years of living in London I'd naturally developed the customary fear of walking alone in the night, but I was so angry that I was willing to take the risk.

I wandered aimlessly through the dark streets, as I did when I needed to calm down. That, however, was not my aim now. No, I didn't want to calm down. I wanted to remain angry while I was on my own too. I wasn't as angry with Ruth as I was with myself; first because I had allowed myself to talk about Cousin Maryam and Uncle Ahmad in such an unguarded way; and second because when Ruth guessed what had happened, I panicked and, to conceal my panic, I overreacted.

I should have explained the ghastly event to Ruth, I should have told her everything. Why didn't I tell her the truth? Clearly I didn't trust her enough. I'd thought that I had no problem in telling her anything but it seemed that no matter how much I trusted her there were still certain things, particularly those which led to family secrets, I couldn't open in front of her. To my astonishment, I realised that I still considered certain matters family secrets, worse still that I was still faithful to the family ethos, that our closet must not be opened in front of strangers. After all these years, I said to myself with regret rather than anger, I was still chained to the family I'd thought I'd disowned a long time ago. Still angry with myself, I decided to go back to Ruth and tell her everything.

I turned and started walking back home but halfway there, I hesitated. I couldn't tell her, and instead of returning to the flat I went into a pub. It was nearly half an hour before closing time but that was long enough for me to down two pints. If I couldn't tell her the whole story I could at least apologise for shouting at her. I could even explain that I wasn't angry with her, only with myself. I was a little tipsy. But I didn't phone Ruth, I dialled Nada's number instead. I didn't know exactly what

I was going to say to her. I hadn't talked to her for nearly two years since that time when Ruth was in Israel. I thought I could pretend that I wanted to talk to Salim but if she sounded her usual flirtatious self I could suggest that we meet, talk and perhaps spend the night together. We could go to a hotel or we could go to another town. I was sure that Nada wouldn't agree to come out at this time of night, not this way, not when she hadn't heard from me for so long. But nor was I sure that I really wanted her to. I wanted to do the outrageous; something that spelt self-destruction. For doing what I'd thought of doing with Nada would certainly have brought my life with Ruth to an end, and such an end would mean a self-inflicted failure. It was as if I wanted to see how it would feel to lose the person with whom I had shared years of my life.

I dialled the number not knowing exactly what I was going to say to Nada. To my relief, Salim answered. He immediately realised that I was drunk and he laughed. He himself sounded as though he had had one too many: "Oh, Ibrahim, come over here and let's continue boozing together!" he said cheerfully.

"I don't want to bother you at this time of night, particularly at home." I was happy that he'd invited me though. That was exactly what I wanted, to be with someone, a friend or a sort of a friend. I didn't want to go back home and face Ruth, but nor did I want to stagger into a late night affair with Nada.

"Don't worry! Nada and Ahmad are in Damascus."

"Really!" I couldn't help feeling let down. I wanted to see Nada. Actually I wanted her to see me, to see me in this state and realise that my relationship with Ruth, or the English woman as she called her, was not going well. I wanted her attention.

"Are they on holiday?" I asked.

"Come over and I'll tell you all about it," he insisted, implying that he was more in need of company than I was.

I had a whisky and went. By the time I arrived, Salim was as drunk as I was. Unshaven, he opened the door dressed only in his vest and pyjama bottoms. The house was in a mess; clothes were lying over the armchairs, unwashed plates and cups were cluttering the coffee-table in the sitting room; the television was left on because it seemed that nobody had bothered to switch it off. On the floor were a glass and a half-empty bottle of whisky.

I couldn't help being puzzled. As far as I knew, Salim's flat was always spotlessly clean. Both Salim and Nada were so meticulous about appearances that they made one think they had no other occupation but to look tidy and be hygienic. I wanted to ask him what had happened but before I did he started talking. He talked about marriage, giving me a long-winded lecture whose conclusion was that marriage in "our culture" had become as bankrupt an institution as it had in the West. Salim, like my other Arab friends in England, still talked about the West as if it were another planet. I couldn't help being amused not only because of this, but also, as I gradually realised, because he was really trying to inform me that Nada had left him.

Like the rest of us in that old, small circle of friends, Salim couldn't talk about personal matters without placing them in a general and theoretical context. We thought we were meant to be intellectuals who had no time to worry ourselves and others with the details of our dull, private affairs. But, the fact of the matter was, we did not trust each other enough, nor were we close enough, to share the intimate details of our personal lives.

I was irritated that Salim still talked that way though he was drunk enough to drop all pretence and inhibitions. Longing for him to get to the point, I was tempted to interrupt his endless babble with, "So what you are saying is, the bitch has run away with another man!" I was drunk enough to say it, but he didn't give me the chance.

"Arab women who live in the West want it both ways," he went on. "They want to remain eastern women but at the same time enjoy the rights of western women."

"What's happened exactly?" I asked. I was both irritated and intrigued to know the scandalous details.

But Salim was determined to continue being vague. He went on lecturing me on the history of marriage, and he didn't stop until he saw that I had dozed off. Eventually he told me what had happened.

Yes, Nada had left him – she'd taken the child and gone, but to my disappointment, she had not run away with a lover. No she'd gone back to her family in Damascus.

It seemed that for years she'd been threatening to leave. Now she'd done it. She had never been content, always demanding new things, especially the things which her eldest sister possessed. She was married to a rich Syrian business man – with whose friend it was rumoured Nada had had an affair. Nada was madly envious of their St John's Wood house and their frequent change of furniture and cars.

"My sister has bought herself yet another new car," she would complain to Salim, "while I don't even have an old one."

Salim would dismiss this with, "We can't afford it."

He was constantly worried about losing his job and the ensuing threat of poverty. But he was not poor. As long as I had known him he had always had a well-paid job. He often boasted that he was always careful to save at least one third of his income. So he could easily have bought Nada a car, and Nada knew that very well.

"Yes we can," Nada would argue, "but you are too mean to part with your money!"

"You don't need a car," he would ignore her remark about his meanness. "You don't work and you don't need to drive to do the shopping. Safeways is just around the corner."

And he always insisted that he wouldn't touch his savings unless it was absolutely necessary. "What if one day we had to run away? What would we do? At least we would have some cash," he told her.

"You Palestinians are always thinking of running away!" she replied sarcastically. Nada was Syrian and always made fun of Salim's anxieties. Salim, a Palestinian from a refugee camp, couldn't help anticipating the worst. The thought of us all being rounded up one day and shot or deported was such an ever-present fear for him that it practically determined whether he should buy a new shirt or not.

"Yes, and with good reason," he would say sternly.

She couldn't argue with that. But neither did she stop complaining.

The real trouble had started when Salim decided to pay for his youngest brother's education. Ali was in his final year of university and up till then Wesaam, Salim's eldest brother, had been taking care of his expenses. But that particular year Wesaam had suffered some financial difficulties and therefore he asked Salim if he could pay. Salim agreed. Having never paid a penny for Ali, Salim thought it only fair that he should pay for at least that final year. When Nada found out she went berserk.

"You don't buy me a car but you give money to your family!"

Salim tried to reason with her but she wouldn't drop the subject and warned, "If you go ahead and give the money to your brother then I shall take Ahmad and go back to my family!"

Salim didn't take her seriously. She'd made such a threat many times before but within a few days she had calmed down and seen sense so he went ahead, transferring the required amount to Ali's account. The next day Nada left the house. She went to stay with her sister in St. John's Wood and three weeks later she flew to Syria taking young Ahmad with her.

"When did all this happen?" I tried to sound shocked but of course I wasn't, I wasn't even surprised. There was nothing unusual about Nada's "either-me-or-your-family". How often had I heard wives of friends giving such an ultimatum? I wondered whether Ruth could say that to me one day. But then I wasn't attached to my family the way Salim was. And anyway Ruth wasn't that kind of woman.

"When did she go to Damascus?"

"Nearly two months ago," Salim replied.

"Really? I didn't know that."

"No, you didn't." His voice was growing subtly reproachful, "You've been too busy to ask after your friends."

"I'm sorry, I've been working hard on a film project."

"A film project?" he said in disbelief. "More like your English girlfriend is keeping you away from us."

"No, it's nothing to do with my girlfriend but ..."

"Aziz saw you with her once," he interrupted. "He said that she's good looking. He said she doesn't look very English."

"Look, it's nothing to do with her," I replied abruptly. I didn't want to start talking about Ruth.

"So why don't you introduce us to her? Why have you been staying away from us?"

"Look I told you, I've been busy with a film. And anyway, the important thing now is you. How are you coping?" I asked, half sincerely. I wanted him to forget about Ruth.

"I don't know," he answered.

"Look, why don't you go to Syria? Try to reason with her or, better still, talk to her family!"

"Talk to her family? Are you joking?"

The implication was that I should have known Nada's family well enough not to make such a suggestion. It was possible that he'd told me something about them once, what greedy bastards they were.

"It was her family who turned her against me. They

were the ones who insisted that she should ask for a divorce if I went ahead and gave my brother the money."

I wanted to say that he and Nada had no future together but I remained silent. We both remained silent. We were both exhausted and had no desire to continue talking.

I stayed the night at Salim's. Lying in bed, in the guest room, I thought how lucky I was to have a woman like Ruth. She'd never wanted a car or a larger flat or anything else: she was content with whatever we had. She never intervened in how I spent my money, she never made any demands. How lucky I was. I decided to return home first thing in the morning, apologise and ask her to marry me. But I forgot all about my decision until it was too late; we had gone back to fighting again.

15

First Barak won the election. Then Ruth and I made more than one effort to revive our relationship, and we started talking about having a child. Actually I didn't talk, she opened the subject.

We had finished our dinner. She had made chicken risotto, which I liked, and we had just cleared the table and were set to finish our wine and watch television.

"Why don't we have a child?" she asked out of the blue.

I looked at her to see how serious she was. She knew that I didn't want children. "Is that why you cooked that delicious chicken risotto?" I teased trying to turn her proposal into a joke.

"Yes it's a bribe," she replied and laughed. "It would be amazing," she said after a pause, in a dreamy voice.

"Yes. It would be amazing trouble!" I said sarcastically.

"Why do you say that?"

I could tell from her voice how hurt she was but she tried not to show it.

"Because you know what I think about having children ..."

"Yes, yes, I know," she interrupted impatiently. "The world is such an awful place, people are so horrible that one shouldn't commit the crime of parenthood. I know, I know what you think. You sound so juvenile sometimes."

"You didn't think I was juvenile when I first told you what I thought," I replied calmly.

"I didn't say anything then because you had had such a hard childhood that it was understandable you didn't want children."

"So what's changed? You no longer believe I had a hard childhood?"

"No! I didn't mean that," she said hesitantly. "I just thought our relationship had reconciled you with your past, that you are now less doubtful about having children."

"It hasn't and I'm not," I said, but fearing that my vehemence might make her think that our relationship had had no major effect on me, I added: "It has changed a lot of things. Many things in my life have changed for the better, but I don't think the world itself has changed."

"So you want us to wait until the world has changed completely?" she asked sarcastically.

"No not the whole world, only my own world." I recalled my old anxiety about being responsible for someone else; tied down, not able to move on or, what concerned me most, to run away. To be crippled by dependents.

"True, I have moved on from that fearful time and world; and the fact that I have managed to survive that dark experience should have made me believe in life, in future generations, however the truth is that the fear of having to hide or run away have never left me. I still don't feel secure enough, nor do I have the faintest idea how I could feel secure enough to have children. I remember Nada saying to Salim, 'You Palestinians are obsessed with running away!' She was right."

"Don't you think I understand?" She sounded sympathetic but not altogether convinced. It seemed that what I'd said had touched her but was she being sympathetic about me or about herself? I wondered, and decided not to answer her question. Ruth, however, was too perceptive and sensitive not to pick up on my deliberate silence.

"What?"

"What?" I replied irritatingly, "you understand what I'm talking about?"

"Of course," she looked at me inquiringly. "I understand more than anybody else. I am Jewish, don't forget!"

"For God's sake!"

"What? What do you mean?"

"You belong to a state which has the nuclear bomb, for God's sake!" I blurted out. At long last I had had the courage to say what I had been suppressing for a long time. Surprised, she remained silent for a while and I was surprised at myself for saying such a thing to her.

"Well, it's true, isn't it?" I asked, trying to justify what I had just said. But I knew that I was only trying to stifle a sudden sense of regret. "You can't understand the constant fear of running and hiding if you belong to a strong state."

"I thought you didn't like us to talk like that?" she said disappointed.

"No, I don't, and we shouldn't, but there are facts which we shouldn't ignore. If things went wrong for us here, you could very easily run back home. I couldn't."

"Yes, that's true! But you no longer have that fear, I can see that. Anybody can see it."

She was right, of course. Living in London for such a long time had actually made the thought of running and hiding feel more like a remembered fear. It was a past fear projected onto the present with the aim of preventing me from forgetting what I had been through. It was dangerously thoughtless to get too comfortable, to take things for granted.

It was guilt too. Realising how secure my life had become in comparison with the lives of my relatives and friends, back there, I couldn't help feeling guilty. And in order to increase my sense of guilt I resorted to thinking that my life was not as secure as it felt and that at any time I might have to run and hide.

Ruth grasped that and was sympathetic.

The next time we discussed having a child she was more forthcoming in confronting the worries I had voiced.

"But there's something else too, isn't there," she said. "I mean the thing that really frightens you about having a child."

"No!"

"Yes!" she replied sternly. "The story about Nada — you're worried that I would do the same?"

"What do you mean?"

I knew exactly what she meant, and she was right.

"You're frightened that I would do the same. That if we had a child I'd take it and run away to Israel."

"No!" I protested, and felt as if I were shaking off a nasty suspicion of mine which had long been on my mind but which I had never dared express until now. "No," I went on denying, "what makes you think that?"

"Because you don't trust me," she said defiantly.

"What?"

I was shocked, though I didn't know if it was because she was making such an accusation or because I realised that it was true. Yes, she was right, I didn't trust her, at least not enough to have a child with her. I feared that when things came to an end between us, which I was becoming increasingly certain of, she would take the child and go to Israel. I wouldn't be able to do anything about it. I felt ashamed of such a suspicion but, as if to console myself, started questioning her, "How about you?" I asked, "you don't trust me either!"

"Yes I do," she replied firmly.

"Really? Why?"

"Because I love you," she said simply.

"I love you too, but love is not a good-enough basis for trust. Sometimes you love people whom you least trust."

I immediately regretted my words for what she'd actually meant to say was that she was willing to take the risk of trusting me. It was something that should have made me appreciate her, but I was in no mood to have any gracious feelings towards her.

I was becoming feverish and felt as if I actually hated her and over the following few days I imagined her in a scene in which she was crying hysterically. She was holding a baby boy, our baby boy, and answering the telephone at the same time. I could hear her screaming, "No that's impossible! It can't be! I talked to her only yesterday! Impossible, my God, no! When did that happen?"

When she began to sob, I rushed towards her, obviously worried that she might collapse, wanting to hold her, to calm her down, but I didn't. I only took the baby from her. The baby was crying and I carried him into the bedroom, away from his hysterical mother. I had no wish to know what she was crying about. The only thing I wanted was to keep the baby away from her, and to protect him. I was frightened that she might have gone mad and that she would do something awful to my child. I was frightened of her and wanted to get away with the baby.

Delirious, I went on weaving this nightmare. I imagined Ruth crying because she had just been told that her sister Dalya had been killed in a suicide bombing. I thought the reason I rushed to take the baby away from her was because I was actually worried that she might throw him out of the window. I was worried not because I'd assumed that she no longer knew what she was doing but because she actually wanted to kill him. She wanted to kill this Palestinian child of hers, this potential suicide bomber who would grow up to kill her family. I feared that she would kill him out of revenge. Why not? Why wouldn't she confront the frightful fact, right there and then; she'd given birth to a potential terrorist, someone who was destined to grow up and kill her family, kill her? I hallucinated until I felt dizzy and collapsed.

For three days, I had a severe fever. I stayed in bed, repeating in my delirium, "No children, no way!"

Ruth told me all this later. She'd nursed me all through those days. She looked very sad, and after that she never talked about us having a child.

Part Four

16

First the Israelis pulled out of Lebanon and then I couldn't stand watching Ruth getting so excited that her country was, at last, doing the right thing. And so I went to see my old friends.

It was May, and it was hot. Here in London, it was hot, and everybody seemed euphoric, apart from me. Now, while sitting here on the sofa, waiting for Ruth to return from the post office, or so I have convinced myself, I remember that day vividly. Well, I should; lots of things have happened to me recently, but loss of memory is not one of them. Besides, it was only a few months ago.

Summer was here and I hate hot weather. I have always hated hot weather. But you come from a hot country, people kept telling me. So what? I hated hot weather all the same. I especially hated hot weather when people sounded more cheerful than you would expect them to be. Everybody I knew seemed to be joyful; the weather was brilliant and Israel was finally doing the sensible thing and withdrawing from Lebanon.

"They should never have gone there in the first place," Ruth declared with what sounded to me like feigned displeasure. Of course she was as pleased as everybody else, perhaps even more so. Her country was, at last, doing something commendable, so why shouldn't she be cheerful too?

"They should never have gone into the West Bank and Gaza," I was irritated and was trying to spoil her ill-concealed sense of satisfaction.

"No, they shouldn't have," she replied, "but who knows, this could be the start of an Israeli withdrawal from all the occupied territories."

"What, including the West Bank and Gaza? You must be joking!"

"No. It could happen."

"Don't be silly. They are withdrawing from Lebanon because they want to get a firmer grip on the territories."

"What makes you think so?"

Now she was getting upset.

"Because I know that nothing good will come out of all this," I said, not so much out of conviction but because I felt more comfortable being gloomily sceptical.

After that neither of us said anything. She went to the study and I decided to see Ahmad and Aziz, of all people. I wanted to consolidate that gloomy mood of mine; I felt the need to do something defiant.

I hadn't seen Ahmad and Aziz for a long time. Since Ruth and I had been together, I had only met them on a few occasions and mostly when it couldn't be avoided. Salim used to give me their news and from what he'd said I gathered that they were still the same.

And that's exactly what I found out for myself when I met them in the late afternoon of that day.

They were all there, Ahmad, Aziz, Salim, and two new fellows whom, I gathered after I had a chance to talk to them, were meant to substitute for Hani and me as the audience which Ahmad and Aziz needed. They were in the same Hammersmith pub where they usually met after work, drinking and chatting. The pub, just like the old friends, didn't seem to have changed at all. To my disappointment, they were as happy as anybody else that I had met that day, only for different reasons. They too were celebrating the Israeli withdrawal from Lebanon but as "a victory for the resistance who drove them out."

"This," Ahmad declared euphorically, "ought to be a good lesson for our cowardly leaders who are going round begging the Americans and the Israelis to give them back a few inches of our land. I hate to admit it, but Hezbollah has proved that we have got it wrong all along. We shouldn't have given up on the intifada!"

I wanted to tell him that what he should actually say was that Hezbollah had proved him right. He had never believed in negotiating with the Israelis, and he had never given up on the intifada. I preferred to remain silent though. The moment I had heard them calling the Israeli withdrawal a victory for Hezbollah, I decided not to get involved in the debate. What he was saying, I realised, was meant to end any possible debate and was a clear signal to me not to express a different view or even to say anything at all.

I was no longer welcome among them. It was clear that they were no longer comfortable in my presence. The way they talked, and agreed with one another, was meant to exclude me or at the very least make my attempts to join in the conversation sound like a sudden, and largely, irrelevant contribution.

At first I felt insulted. I thought of responding rudely, but I thought I should explain, if only indirectly, that what had driven me away from them were their rigid and archaic views. But that would not have been fair. Regardless of whether I was right or wrong, I'd made my choice and left them; for years I stayed away and they had got used to the idea that I was no longer one of them. I had no right to be there, or to break in on their little meeting and compel them to make concessions for my sake. I'd become a mere intruder.

I considered leaving and disappearing, but where would I go? Back to Ruth? Back to listening to her expressing, with undisguised smugness, relief that her country had at last done the right thing? Yes, Ruth, I'm running away from you. I wondered whether she knew that; I wondered what she would feel if she realised that I'd come to see this old group of friends just to keep away from her. We had reached a point where we both had realised that we couldn't turn back and make things better. The best we could hope for was to keep out of each other's way or even each other's sight. No, I couldn't go home; I couldn't go back to Ruth.

I could go to another pub, but I would have to sit on my own and I couldn't bear the idea of being alone, especially then. No, I needed company. I needed to be with someone.

I tried to talk to Salim, to start a one-sided conversation with him which had nothing to do with politics. I had noticed that he hadn't said a word. He was withdrawn, oblivious to everything going on. Now that I looked closely at him I could see he was in bad shape. He looked even worse than when I'd visited him at home. I assumed that Nada hadn't come back and that he'd taken to drinking. I was about to ask him how things were but Aziz, guessing that I was about to speak to Salim, raised his hand indicating that I'd better leave him alone.

I looked at Aziz inquiringly, but with Salim present, he couldn't say anything. Holding his nearly empty glass he got up and walked towards the bar. He wanted to buy another round but, I assumed, he also wanted me to follow him. At the bar he insisted on buying me a pint even though I hadn't finished mine.

"What's the matter?" I asked.

"He's in a bad way," Aziz said, preparing me for a long story.

"I know!" I replied, implying that I knew the story, that even if I hadn't been seeing my old friends, I still knew what was happening to them, "Nada has taken the child and left him."

"Is that all you know?" He was contemptuous. I might know something, but obviously not enough.

"What else is there to know?"

"He nearly ended in Palestine Branch," Aziz said, putting it bluntly as if to shock me deliberately.

"What?" I was shocked, "In Syria?"

"How many Palestine Branches do you know?" he replied sarcastically. "Yes, in Syria. He went there to make it up with his wife but her family tried to get him arrested and thrown into prison." Aziz paused to gulp down the last of his pint.

"And what happened?"

"He asked Nada to come back with him, but she refused. She only wanted a divorce. He tried to frighten her; he threatened that if she insisted on a divorce he would take the child back to London." Aziz looked pleased that he was telling me something I hadn't heard before and that I was so curious about. He didn't really care much about Salim's troubles except as a topic for gossip. He despised Salim's attitude towards Nada. Salim had been too soft on her and that was why she'd been able to give him such a hard time, or "to ride him" as Aziz preferred to say. Aziz firmly believed that a man mustn't get married unless he knows how to handle a wife properly. He often boasted that his own wife wouldn't dare take one step out of the house without his permission.

"He was only trying to scare some sense into her so she would come back with him," he continued, "but you see her family didn't want that to happen. According to Salim they were the ones who were encouraging her to keep demanding a divorce. When they knew he was threatening to deprive her of seeing the child they tried to get him arrested and thrown into jail."

"What? They complained to the police?"

"What police?" Aziz asked impatiently. "I told you, they wanted him locked up in Palestine Branch. They contacted the Mukhabarat."

"What? But what does the Mukhabarat have to do with domestic problems?" I couldn't believe what he was saying. "That's absurd!"

"Everything is absurd in that country," he was amused that I was so shocked at what he was telling me. "You see, her cousins know people in the Mukhabarat. They contacted them and told them that Salim was an Israeli spy. He'd come to Syria pretending that he was coming to solve his problems with his wife when in fact he was on a spying mission."

"What? But how could they do that?"

"They wanted to get rid of him," he replied as if he was stating a simple matter of fact.

"But he's their son-in-law." I didn't really know what to say in response to what he was telling me. Actually at that moment I was no longer thinking of Salim. I'd started thinking of Ruth and me, recalling the argument we had had when we thought – to be precise, when Ruth thought – we ought to have a child. I remembered my fear of Ruth doing what Nada had done and I started imagining myself going through what Salim had been through. I imagined Ruth had taken the child and gone back to Israel and then I'd followed her there, broken hearted, begging her to come back, to bring my child back. But she wouldn't listen and when I insisted she, no, her sister Edith – she's the one who hated me most – would try to get me arrested. She would call the police or security forces and tell them I was a Palestinian terrorist. Mind you, an Israeli prison is a lot easier than Palestine Branch; I interrupted my dark imagination, mockingly. I wanted to stop these thoughts.

"But, what about the child? What about Ahmad?" I asked, not that I expected Aziz to know. I just wanted to go back to Salim's misfortune. "I mean if they cared about the son so much that they wanted him to stay with his mother, how could they try to do this to his father."

"What are you talking about? They don't care. Besides the boy is too young to understand what's been happening"

"But one day he will know what they tried to do and he'll take it out on his mother or his mother's family." I was actually thinking of Edith, thinking of how she would have tried to get me arrested.

"What! You've obviously lived here too long and have forgotten how to understand these people. They don't care. They don't care about the child or the mother or anybody! They just want to have it their own way."

"I know that they didn't approve of Nada marrying Salim in the first place." Salim had told me that. It wasn't that they thought him not good enough for their daughter but rather they preferred that she return to Syria. Nada didn't want to go back, she wanted to live in London. She was still young and didn't want to waste her youth in miserable Syria.

"And what happened next," I asked, "I mean how did Salim get away?"

"How do you expect? When he knew what they were plotting he took the first flight back to London."

"Poor man!"

"What a humiliation!" Aziz said, with a look of contempt, rather than sympathy, on his face.

"Yes, but there's something worse than the humiliation."

"What?"

"It's possible that he won't see his son again."

He nodded.

"Yes, as long as Nada insists on divorcing him and as long as she stays in Syria, Salim and his son might never see each other again." I was trying to elaborate the problem. I wanted Aziz to become sympathetic. "Salim wouldn't dare set foot in Syria again and his son couldn't travel on his own, not now anyway, not until he's much older and then he might not be able to, or possibly even want to."

Aziz nodded. He looked bored, but I decided to go on nevertheless. "He might not want to see his father. You see, by then his mother could have led him to believe that his father doesn't want him, that he has given up on them, that it was his father who forced them to go back to Syria so he could get rid of them both. A woman like Nada is capable of anything."

"She is," Aziz agreed.

The bitch! I felt so sorry for Salim. I felt sorry for him and ashamed of myself. That plotting bitch, I thought, and at the same time grew angry with myself. As if to make it up to Salim I wanted to find a way to put things right.

"Doesn't he know anybody in Syria who could help him?" I asked.

Aziz shook his head: "He doesn't know anybody apart from his wife and her family. He's only been there a few times and only because he was married to her."

"What about Syrians who live over here?" I asked.

"Nobody!" Aziz replied. His lazy voice implied that he'd

thought of this himself but to no avail. "The Syrians he knows here are as helpless as he is. Most cannot go back themselves. You know the kind of people Salim mixes with."

Yes, I knew. I knew his friends well enough to feel sorry for him.

"He's been a hard-working man." For the first time Aziz was showing admiration for Salim, "He's known how to look after himself but he hasn't been ambitious enough to meet important people."

"True!" I said, "I remember how happy he was when Nada agreed to marry him. At the beginning she didn't want him. He didn't have enough money and she wanted to be rich like her sister. She eventually agreed because the calculating bitch realised that her chances of getting married were diminishing."

Nada was growing older and for her, an Arab woman living in London, finding someone to marry was becoming increasingly difficult. She knew only a few Arab families, and her choice of husbands was limited. She was still living with her sister and brother-in-law. They had just started making money and they couldn't help noticing the envious look on Nada's face. They wanted to get rid of her, and thought that she should go back to Damascus where she would probably find a suitable husband. She had finished her studies and it was about time she went back home.

But Nada didn't want to go back. The years she'd spent living and studying in London were the happiest of her life. She wanted to stay and get rich. Marrying Salim was her way of staying in London without the risk of growing old as a spinster. Salim was happy when she at last accepted him and was willing to do anything to please her. But he wasn't rich nor ambitious enough to become rich and so he never won her respect. She made impossible demands and cheated on him. Poor Salim!

Aziz went back to the table to join the others but I wanted to be alone for a while. Poor Salim, I thought of taking him home with me. He needed to be around people and couldn't stay alone in that flat of his. Yes, I must take him with me, but then I remembered Ruth and immediately dropped the hospitable impulse.

It wasn't that Ruth would have objected to having Salim. No, she would have welcomed the idea and tried to be as hospitable as she could. No one, I thought, could be more compassionate towards people in distress than Ruth. The problem was that I didn't want Salim to discover her identity. I was still terrified that any of my old friends might find out that I was living with an Israeli. Of course I was being cowardly but I preferred to be a coward rather than face the hostility of people I knew. I was sure that some of them would suspect Ruth of being a Mossad agent; I myself would be seen as someone with dubious associations and could lose my job and end up being snubbed by most Palestinians and Arabs in London. A few might be sympathetic and even appreciate my courage, but they wouldn't lift a finger to help me nor would they want to be seen to be close to me. Cowards, I thought, and finished my pint. I bought another and drank half of it in one go. I kept drinking until I felt that my feet might no longer carry me.

I made my way back to the table rather unsteadily and sat by Salim. He smiled and looked as if he was trying to read what was going through my mind. They all looked as if they wanted to know what I was thinking, to know my secret. Ruth was my secret, but I felt I should no longer have any secrets in my life. Yes, I must put an end to it.

That night I went back home determined to end everything, to ask Ruth to leave, or leave myself. Yes, I must leave, I thought, totally drunk, that's the best way out, to throw a few clothes into a suitcase and leave right now. But what do I tell Ruth? I asked myself. I tell her nothing, I just pack some clothes and leave. I was determined.

When I arrived home Ruth was asleep. The sitting room was tidy but in the study I noticed the cluttered desk; scattered papers and open dictionaries, unfolded newspapers and an empty glass of wine. She must have been working hard, so hard that she could no longer keep her eyes open, and only then did she go to bed. I couldn't help imagining her, sitting at the desk, bending over newspapers and dictionaries, translating, reading the original text in Hebrew, looking up words in dictionaries, weighing them up in her mind, constructing one sentence after another, and writing them down in English. I imagined her working with dedication but feeling sad at what had happened that evening and what had been happening to us for some time.

I tried to read what she had translated but was too

drunk to focus. I could only see the words, the letters, in her handwriting, clean and neat; nothing crossed out. It was the handwriting of someone relaxed and confident, someone who wasn't bothered about anything or anybody. No, Ruth wasn't sad, she wasn't troubled at all. The feeling of sympathy, which I had felt for her as I imagined her working, vanished.

Ruth was confident and happy. And why shouldn't she be? I remembered our early discussions, how optimistic and happy she was. I decided to go into the bedroom, pack my clothes and leave. Yes, I'll go into the bedroom and make as much noise as I like and if she wakes up, which I hoped she would, I'll tell her I'm leaving. I don't want this relationship any more, I'm leaving.

Ruth was sleeping soundlessly which like her neat handwriting, was a sign of an untroubled conscience, of a relaxed and happy soul. I felt more annoyed. For a second or two I considered picking up a pillow, putting it against her face and pressing down hard, pressing down against her nose and mouth until she was as breathless as she was soundless. But then she turned, I could see her face now. I looked at her, it wasn't the face of a relaxed and happy person, but of an unhappy, exhausted person. I quietly closed the door, and went back to the sitting room. I can't leave, I can't leave her, I said to myself.

17

First the Camp David talks failed then we discovered that ours was a doomed relationship. The end, in other words, was approaching. I decided to write Ruth a letter.

Dear Ruth,
I've been having dark thoughts. I don't wish to frighten you but we must do something before these dark thoughts become frightful actions. I think it's about time that we faced painful facts.

After meeting each other seven years ago, and living together for five years, we must admit that from the beginning our love was hopeless. We were two lonely people who wrongly believed that they were on their own because they had been waiting for the right person. We both believed in the existence and possible arrival of the right person. We are a Palestinian and an Israeli who met in the early euphoric days of treaty-signing and a peace process. Our relationship was based on an undeclared treaty to be in love with one another or, to be more precise, to act out that we were in love; that's it, it's a treaty of love between a Palestinian man and an Israeli woman. And just like the many treaties that have been signed between the Palestinians and Israelis, it was awkward and shaky, too late or too early: too late to be unprecedented and a taboo-breaker, and too early to become just another relationship between two people from two different backgrounds. You and I have just been playing at Palestinians and Israelis. We must have realised this only a short time after moving in together. First there was the acute sense of being too near each other for too long, which resulted in those moments of silence. Then came the boredom. Our relationship was not meant to become dull and predictable. We obviously didn't want to give up, not that early anyway. Why? Because we were frightened of acknowledging failure and of leaving. When it came to relationships we both knew how unsuccessful we had been. We also hated leaving, neither of us had the courage to leave or to take the first step towards leaving. On the few occasions when I've felt we should end it I thought of leaving myself rather than telling you to do so, of taking some clothes and going to live in a hotel. But that sounded more like having a break from each other rather than leaving for good. And do you remember when we had that huge row? It was so terrible that the fear of leaving vanished – yet still I couldn't suggest separation.

You asked me if I wanted you to leave. Of course you didn't mean it, but our row had become so ferocious that only a devastating suggestion could put an end to it. I think you were also making this suggestion to make it easier for me. I said no; not only did I not want you to leave but I also didn't want to hear the question of you leaving.

"No!" I yelled, and as if I were escaping a blazing fire that was about to consume the place, I tore out of the flat. But now I think we must face the painful reality and split up – and if you would ask whether you should leave I would say it's for the better. My dark thoughts are frightening me and I think your leaving would put an end to them…

No, I said to myself and stopped writing. No I said, and tore up the letter and rushed out of the flat. Once I was in the street I walked briskly and aimlessly, trying to lose the sound of my own words.

I kept walking and walking until eventually I was exhausted and then decided to go and see Salim. I hadn't seen him since meeting him on that occasion in the pub. I'd intended to see him but kept postponing it. Now I felt was the appropriate time to see him again; his life with Nada was ruined and mine with Ruth was going the same way. Our common failure might provide us with some consolation.

Salim was in a worse state than I'd anticipated. The house was tidy, though not as spotlessly clean as it used to be when Nada was still there. Salim was shaven and dressed in clean clothes. He wasn't drinking and he tried, at least at first, to sound sober and composed. Rather than telling me what had been happening in his own life he started talking about politics. I'd assumed that he had more pressing personal concerns to contend with and nor was he the sort of person who passionately held political convictions.

"It was bound to fail," Salim sounded as if he had nothing to worry about other than the recent negotiations between the Israelis and Palestinians.

I tried to ignore his remark, hoping that he would start talking to me about his own problems.

"These negotiations were doomed from the start. You cannot negotiate with people who are occupying your land and subjugating your people to their will; you can only fight them."

He made this statement with surprising certainty. This was not Salim talking, this was Ahmad or Aziz, and I felt doubly annoyed. I was annoyed because he insisted on talking about politics, and also because he was parroting the same old rhetoric. I made no response hoping that he would change the subject. But he didn't let up.

"Our leaders have let us down once again! They've sold out, they've given up on the intifada for nothing but their personal gains," he went on and on until I felt I could take no more.

"Since when have you been so interested in politics?" My voice unwittingly took on a sarcastic tone.

He looked disturbed. Up till a few minutes earlier I'd shown nothing but sympathy and compassion, I'd nodded and smiled even though I obviously didn't agree with him, but all of a sudden I became sarcastic.

"Why shouldn't I be so interested in politics?" he asked, irritated. "Why shouldn't all of us? You see, that's our problem, you and me and most Palestinians, we are never interested enough in politics. And if we show any interest at all, it turns out to be just talk. We sit in cafes and pubs and talk. We drink pints of beer and talk, moan about this and that. We never do anything."

For a moment I was sure he was merely mimicking

Ahmad and Aziz, but I instantly realised that this couldn't be what he had heard from them; for he was being critical of his two faithful friends too. Ahmad and Aziz were, after all, the sort of people who sat in pubs, talked and complained, while pouring pints of lager down their throats. This was new and strange, and I couldn't help being surprised.

"We are only interested in our personal gains and worries," he went on, his voice adopting a preaching tone. "We say that we care about the suffering of our people under Israeli occupation, but when do we care? In our spare time? When there is no profit to be made somewhere else?"

Well put, Imam Salim! I wanted to respond but the sincerity in his voice was too clear to permit such a sardonic remark. "I'm glad you're saying this because you, of all people, have every reason to be totally taken up by your own personal affairs. It's very brave of you to forget your own problems and concentrate on the suffering of the people as a whole."

"That's what we should all do," he replied immediately, looking at me to see whether I was being serious or just making fun of him. "What are our personal problems in comparison to the suffering of those living in refugee camps? Our personal suffering is nothing, nothing at all, nothing, we are all nothing, nothing."

He began to cry and went on crying like a child.

"I've lost my job," he sobbed.

"Really? When?" I asked. I wasn't surprised at all, but I wanted him to stop crying.

"Three weeks ago." He took a tissue out of his pocket and started wiping his tears.

I had expected him to get fired. I had expected that to happen earlier than it actually did. But Salim had had an understanding boss. He himself, it seemed, had gone through a rough time in his own marriage and therefore felt that Salim ought to be given a chance while he dealt with his problems. Salim was grateful and promised to sort himself out as soon as possible. But he didn't. His boss warned him several times but Salim was in no state to heed any warning. Eventually his boss could no longer tolerate him coming in late, his shabby look and his drunkenness.

It sounded to me as if Salim wanted to get fired, to have more problems. He was heading towards self-destruction and I felt that I must stay with him, at least for that evening. I also wanted to stay away from Ruth. I wanted to avoid going back and not be reminded of the fact that our relationship was going nowhere. For a moment I wished to tell him about my own problems, but couldn't.

"Let's go out," I suggested instead, trying to be cheerful, "you need to get out. I'm sure you haven't eaten."

He nodded. "I have no appetite though."

"All right, we'll go to the pub first," I said. "We'll have a couple of pints and that should give you an appetite."

"No, I don't want to drink. Soon I'm going out to meet somebody, and I don't want to smell of alcohol."

"What is it? A job interview?" I asked encouragingly.

"A job interview? Now?" he replied, pointing to the darkness outside. "What kind of a job interview would that be?"

"A night watchman?" I replied and laughed. I hoped that he would too.

"It's not a job interview," he said curtly.

"Then it must be a woman," I said, as if insisting on cheering him up, "you don't want to drink to impress her with your good manners."

"No, it's a man, a friend, someone from the Islamic Movement," he said sternly, and looked at me pointedly to see the effect his answer would have on me.

And yes, I was taken by surprise, exactly as he must have expected me to be. I couldn't believe that Salim of all people would be associating himself with members of the Islamic Movement, or for that matter, with any organisation. Salim had never cared enough about politics to join a political party, and his love of drinking was so strong that it was sure to keep him very distant from anything religious.

I was startled but still I tried to conceal it, "Why do you want to see him?" I was hoping that he'd tell me there was nothing too dubious about it, that it was purely a sociable meeting,

"I need a spiritual guide," he said simply and innocently as if he were announcing that he was going to Safeways to buy some cheese. "I need someone to show me where my life has gone so wrong. The brother I'm going to meet tonight is going to guide me back onto the right path."

I couldn't believe what I was hearing, and stared at him, hoping that at any moment he would burst out laughing and tell me that I'd been had, that this was only a joke. But the look of sincerity didn't leave his face. I realised the matter was a lot worse than I could ever have imagined. I saw him going way beyond my reach, disappearing.

"Look! Obviously you need somebody to talk to," I said. "Why don't you talk to Ahmad or Aziz, or any of your other friends?"

"They have no time for me," he replied sadly. "They're only interested in their own personal lives. No one has ever bothered to listen to me, let alone offer help and support. The few times I have tried to open up to them, they were either embarrassed or bored."

I thought he was exaggerating, that he must have received some support but had expected more. When he didn't get it, he started thinking that they didn't care.

"That's not true!" I objected, "I've always listened to you."

"You, Ibrahim?" he replied with a grin on his face.

"Yes, I have!" I said and, realising that that was not really true went on, "And if in the past I didn't offer help, well I'm willing to start helping you now."

"You've enough problems of your own to contend with," he said, the grin still on his face.

"Yes, that's true." Alert to the fact that he knew I had problems, I added hesitantly, "That's why I know how important it is to share your problems with a friend."

"Yes, but you've never shared your problems with me or with any of your friends," he replied reproachfully, "you've never even told us that you have troubles."

I didn't know what to say. It was strange to see how the moment he started talking about me he quickly became sober and self-confident.

181

"You want to help me," he said, grinning once more and shaking his head as if he thought I was being foolish, "yet for years you've avoided us as if we were diseased, all for the sake of your Israeli woman."

"How did you know she's Israeli?" Shocked as I was, I still considered the possibility of denying that Ruth was Israeli.

"Everybody knows that," he replied calmly, "do you think you can hide something like that for long?"

"But I thought you'd always believed that she's English?" I hadn't woken up from the shock.

"Well, at first we thought she was English," he said in such a neutral voice that he may as well have been talking about a distant relative, "but when you stopped coming, we were puzzled. We didn't think that having an English girlfriend was the reason. We didn't expect you to distance yourself from us. No, we thought that you would introduce her to us, if only for the sake of showing off. You know how many of us feel proud when they have an English woman. People got suspicious about you and one day someone said that your partner was Israeli and we all thought that that must be it then, that's why he's been keeping away from us: he's embarrassed or even ashamed. Some agreed that you should be."

I sat there listening to Salim and tried to remember the times I had seen my old friends, to recall their reactions. I remembered the last time I had met them in the pub, the way they had tried to exclude me from the conversation and, generally, their distant attitude towards me. Now that I understood I wanted to tell Salim that I didn't abandon them because of Ruth. I particularly wanted to make it clear to him that I'd never been ashamed or embarrassed of my relationship with Ruth, that if anything, it was them, the way they thought and talked that prevented me from ever thinking of introducing Ruth to them.

I was getting all worked up inside.

"Look! It's none of your or anybody else's business who I have for a partner," I exclaimed, angrily. "Ruth is not the reason, but the stuffy and stupid way in which you, I don't mean you personally, but the whole lot of you, think and express yourselves. It was that empty repetitive way that made me want to keep away. I wanted something new, something different, I wanted to think differently and look at things in a new way."

Salim listened to me silently which only encouraged me to continue, "I didn't introduce Ruth to you because I wanted her to take me to the new, rather than me dragging her to the old. I wanted to change. Ruth was my way to change. You can tell that to Ahmad and Aziz when they start attacking me again."

But of course it was too late. Salim wasn't going to tell anybody anything. He probably wasn't going to see much of his old friends. In fact he didn't seem that interested in any kind of explanation. It was too late. It was too late even to try to stop him seeing the fundamentalist he was going to meet, but just as I stood up, he said, "I understand."

I looked at him waiting to know what he understood.

"I understand about her, and why you've stayed away

from us. I understand now. I didn't then. But now things are different for me. You wanted a change in your life, that's exactly what I want now."

"I'm glad, but I have to tell you ..." but I couldn't continue. I wanted to tell him how bad things had become between Ruth and me. I wanted to tell him that given my experience of change, change might not be the solution. But after my outburst in defence of Ruth and my search for something new, I couldn't. I had to remain silent.

"What?" he asked.

"Nothing!"

Nothing, and I left. I went home, back to my Israeli woman, to the woman I could no longer call mine without feeling a sad sense of irony, "Ruth, my woman!"

Ruth wasn't home. The flat was tidy and spotlessly clean. For a moment I thought she'd gone, that she'd packed her things and left me for good. But everything, her paintings, photos and books were all there. I went into the bedroom, opened the cupboard and to my relief, yes to my relief, her clothes were still there. She hadn't gone.

But my sense of relief was gradually replaced by disappointment. Yes, she should have done the right thing and left, it would have been great if she had.

I sat in the sitting room, watching television and drinking. But I was only pretending to watch television; I was actually waiting for her. The longer I was on my own the less I was able to concentrate on the television and the more impatient I grew. Eventually I found myself wondering, where is she? Where the hell is she? And I started getting worried that something might have happened to her. I thought of phoning Yael, but no, I shouldn't. I went on drinking.

An hour later she came back. She was smiling as she came into the sitting room, just as if she'd been having a good time, but the moment she saw me, the smile disappeared. She apparently didn't expect me to be back before her.

"Where've you been?"

"Out! Shopping," she said raising her hand in which she was holding two carrier bags of clothes, one from Harvey Nichols and the other from Selfridges.

I was surprised by the casual way she said "shopping" as if she was one of those women who shop every day. I was even more surprised at the way she swung the carrier bags. Ruth never liked shopping, especially for clothes. As long as I had known her she only bought clothes when she needed them. I rarely saw her buying more than one item at a time unless there was an unmissable sale on. It wasn't that she didn't care much about her appearance. She always made sure that she looked elegant but mostly in a practical way. She didn't like anything that was costly or flashy. Neither her modest means nor her desire to be inconspicuous allowed her to buy expensive clothes. Or so I believed until I saw her swinging shopping bags from Harvey Nichols and Selfridges.

"What have you bought?" I asked. What I actually wanted to ask was, "Since when have you become a lady of fashion?"

"A couple of things," she said in the same irritatingly casual tone of voice.

"Did you need them?"

"No, not urgently."

"Since when have you bought your clothes from Harvey Nichols and Selfridges?" I said, eyeing the shopping bags.

"Look! I went out to enjoy myself and I did. So, please, don't start!" And before I could say anything she added, "I'm going to sleep now."

I was simmering with anger. For a moment I thought of grabbing the shopping bags, opening the window and throwing them out, "There! You can go back to Harvey Nichols and Selfridges and enjoy yourself some more!" I would tell her. Then I would throw all her clothes and everything that belonged to her out of the window. I was so angry I wanted to tear off the clothes she was wearing and kick her, naked, out of the flat. I did nothing. I just sat there imagining myself hurting her.

18

First we thought that we should face facts and split up, then she asked me, "Do you want to end it?" So she's been thinking of leaving too, I thought, remembering the letter I had written but had lacked the courage to complete.

"I'm asking you, do you want us to split up?"

It was late evening. She was sitting at the desk in the study. She had been working so hard on her translation that the last thing I expected her to do was to look up at me and ask if I wanted to end it.

Still I wasn't totally surprised. By now we had reached a stage in our deteriorating relationship where we no longer bothered to sit facing one another over a glass of wine or a cup of coffee. I myself had grown so detached that I no longer cared how and when we talked about our problems. I didn't mind whether I'd just come back from work or if she was practically out of the front door. It was the end, I realised, and that evening I wanted to say yes, let's end this partnership, but I was too tired.

I'd just come back; it was late. I'd been staying out late recently. I'd been meeting up with Ahmad and Aziz. I went to see them for the sake of Salim.

"He's falling into the hands of the fanatics and we need to help him," I urged Ahmad and Aziz.

At first they reacted the way I'd expected. "Why are you

taking such an interest in Salim's affairs?" Ahmad asked.

He genuinely didn't seem to understand. They both looked amused and I could just imagine them thinking, for years he's been lying in the arms of his Israeli woman, he's avoided us and now he's the one who's pretending to care about Salim and trying to save him from the fundamentalists.

"I think Salim knows his own interests better than all of us," Ahmad said. Aziz nodded in agreement. They were annoyed too. They didn't like it that I was the one who was showing such interest in Salim. But then they wouldn't have liked it even if I hadn't abandoned them. They essentially didn't like anybody to show any real concern and compassion. Salim was right, I thought after I'd talked to them and failed to get them to help him, these are not the sort of friends who care for you.

They were even too annoyed to notice that my interest in Salim was also an attempt to find my way back into their lives. I wanted to revive my old friendship with them, to be one of them again. It wasn't that I'd changed my mind about them, nor had I become so tolerant as to accommodate their views. It was just that I no longer worried much about it. I just no longer cared.

This was the result of feeling that life with Ruth had no future. She and I were simply stuck in a rut, we couldn't go forwards nor could we undo our relationship and go backwards. The company of Ahmad and Aziz seemed the best temporary alternative to avoid confrontation.

The following morning Ruth asked me the same question: "Do you want us to split up?"

She was exhausted. She'd been working to a deadline and had stayed up all night. I didn't know what she'd been working on, nor did I feel the slightest desire to ask. I wasn't being particularly mean, it was just that for a long time neither of us had shown any interest in what the other was doing. Besides, as she was now asking me whether I wanted to end our relationship, it would have been absurd to ask her what she was translating.

Do you want to end it? Yes, I wanted to say. I wasn't too tired to say it. I was frightened. The thought of being without her, the thought of change, terrified me still. Nor could I bring myself to say no.

"Is that what you want?" I asked instead.

"No, that's not what I want," she replied firmly, "that's what you want, I think."

Ignoring what she said, I asked, "Is there someone else?"

"What?"

"Have you met somebody?" I repeated the question trying to sound as patient as possible. "Yes, because quite frankly if there isn't anybody else I don't think you would dare suggest splitting up."

She stared at me in astonishment, "What are you talking about?" She sounded as if she was trying to appear angry but, understandably enough, she couldn't. What I was saying was absurd and anger, therefore, was pointless: "Is that how you want to carry on with this conversation?"

I looked at her questioningly, pretending that I didn't understand.

"First you ignore my question, and then you accuse me of having someone else because I suggest we should split up!"

"I'm just trying to get to the point," I said.

"No you're not, you're trying to put me on the defensive so I'll forget what I asked you,' she replied firmly.

"But why did you insist on asking the question? Why ask it in the first place if splitting up is not actually what you want."

"Because you look and behave as if you can't stand the sight of me anymore," she replied. "You've been staying out late every night, and when you come back you hardly talk to me."

"It feels the same from where I stand," I said. "You too seem pre-occupied and distant."

"Yes, but I'm not staying out late every night," she pointed out calmly.

"You don't need to stay out late to have someone else." I was irritated by her calmness so returned to manipulating the situation.

"Look!" She sounded determined not to lose her temper, "I don't have someone else, and if I've been pre-occupied and distant it's because I feel that you don't want me to be close to you."

So it's all my fault now, I said to myself, but I wasn't going to let her win. "Why don't you try to be close to me then?" I asked and before giving her a chance to answer, went on: "Why don't you try to find out? Something important has happened to me and on more than one occasion I've wanted to tell you, to share my worries with you, but you don't seem to be interested."

For a moment I felt, or to be honest, wished that she

would reply angrily, protesting that that was not true, but to my disappointment she didn't. She remained calm. She seemed to have realised that I was trying to put her on the defensive again and decided not to fall for it.

"So what's been happening? Are you in some kind of trouble?" she asked with genuine interest.

"No don't worry, I'm not in trouble," I replied, disappointed, "but I don't want to talk about it now."

She said nothing in response. She only stared at me; a stare which meant that she was actually concerned but it was me who didn't want to open up. Eventually I succumbed.

"Look, it's Salim," I said, and told her what had been happening to him.

Ruth hadn't known anything apart from Nada returning to Syria with the child. She didn't even know that I had seen Salim a few times since then. Now that I had told her about Salim, she felt she wanted to meet him. "Why don't you invite him here?" she urged me.

"Invite him here?"

"Yes!"

"Yes, it might be a good idea," I said hesitantly. I was actually trying to think of an excuse without raising her suspicions or hurting her feelings.

"It is a good idea," she affirmed "you say that he's lonely and that it was the lack of friendship that pushed him towards the religious so why don't we give him the friendship he needs. We could introduce him to our friends and perhaps try to help him find a job."

"Yes, that's a good idea," I agreed, but by then I'd found

the excuse: "But, you see it might already be too late. He's already become religious and I don't think he'd feel comfortable in our company."

"He couldn't have changed so much so quickly," she wondered.

"Yes, he could!" I replied, "I've seen it happen before. Friends who for years were into western fashion and music turn religious as fast as moving from one room to another."

"Just like that," she said in a voice which seemed to imply that I was only exaggerating.

"Well, it doesn't actually happen that suddenly. Of course they themselves say that it happens all of a sudden, they come to their senses and discover the right path, the path of God, or whatever they call it. But the actual change happens gradually, it starts while they are still non-religious, sometimes when they are still drinking and obsessed with a Western way of life. They feel guilty and to overcome that guilt they console themselves with the belief that one day they will repent."

And I went on and on, half convincing myself, but determined to make her give up on the idea of inviting Salim.

"Still, I think you should keep trying," she said.

I promised I would try. But I didn't need to fulfill my promise. Two days later Aziz phoned me at the office to tell me that Salim was getting ready to go to Afghanistan.

"Did you hear the latest about your friend Salim?" he asked sarcastically.

"What? No I haven't."

"Well our believing friend is getting himself ready to join the mujahedeen," he laughed.

"What?" I yelled, annoyed more than surprised. I was annoyed that Aziz was laughing while telling me such terrible news. I nearly told him it wasn't funny. I was angry, Salim was not wrong when he said that they were an unreliable bunch of friends, and nearly said so to Aziz but thought this was not a time for fighting.

"Can't we do something about it?" I asked, trying to get him to be serious, "can't we see him and try to persuade him to change his mind."

"Forget it man!" His impatience implied that he'd expected me to say as much. He was probably annoyed that I didn't treat the matter as a joke too, "It's too late anyway."

"Well as long as he hasn't gone there yet, I don't think it's too late."

"Well, you can try," he said with the same impatience, but, after a pause, he added sarcastically, "but you have to go down to the mosque. That's the only place you can get hold of him nowadays."

"I don't mind going to the mosque," I replied, ignoring his sarcasm. There was a pause and then he wished me good luck before hanging up.

What a friend! What bastards, Aziz and the rest! Salim is destroying himself and the only thing they can do is to watch and laugh. But instead of being angry I was content. Their disloyalty to Salim had probably made me feel less ashamed of my disloyalty towards them. I was no more disloyal than they had proved to be. I decided to leave the office right away and see Salim. I shall go to the mosque and try, right there, to convince him not to go to Afghanistan, or at least to postpone his trip for a little longer until he's thought it through. There was still time to think things through calmly.

With much determination I left the office. I took the bus going towards Regent's Park and couldn't help being amused that I was actually going to a mosque. I hadn't been to a mosque for more than twenty-five years. The last time I was in a mosque was just before my brother Fadi died.

Recalling those days, and particularly Fadi's death, I felt near to tears. I decided not to go to see Salim. I got off the bus and went to a pub on Great Portland Street instead.

In the pub with the second large scotch in front of me, I became aware of the real motive behind my fervent interest in Salim. With brutal honesty, I admitted to myself that I didn't care a bit about Salim and his fate. Deep down, I'd very little respect for him; he was a pathetic little man who couldn't even keep a family or a job. His turning back to religion and his decision to go to Afghanistan might be all there was to respect him for. I realised that I was interested in Salim's ensuing misfortune because it sounded like a story, more precisely a script for a film: all the elements were there of a story about a little man who tried to overcome his failure in life by embracing religion and joining people who claimed to be on a universal mission. I could imagine it all, scene after scene, from seeing him lying drunk on the sofa in his messy flat, to being bearded and dressed in an Islamic outfit, heading to Heathrow to catch a plane to Karachi on his way to Afghanistan.

Imagining these scenes, one by one, I felt a great sense of satisfaction, something which I hadn't felt since my early days with Ruth. I liked it now more than I had liked it then. For I'd had very little to feel happy about lately, especially in my work. The magazine for which I worked had been sinking into financial difficulties and had become a fortnightly instead of a weekly. Many people lost their jobs and the rest of us felt less secure than ever. In order to prevent us from asking for a raise, the editor kept warning us that he might move the magazine to Dubai. "Everybody is moving," he kept saying. "It's cheaper to publish there." And he would go on, lecturing us about the unhappy destiny of the Arab migrant media, as if we didn't know. "The Arab media in Europe has had its golden age and now it's come to an end, finished." Threateningly, he reminded us, "People are going back and I don't know how much longer I can convince my sponsors that it's better to stay here."

After ten years of working for this stupid magazine, I realised with a deep sense of disappointment – which after all was, and still is, one of my specialties – that I could lose my job without any hope of finding another unless I went to Dubai. And I didn't want to go to bloody Dubai. I didn't want to go anywhere. Making a film about Salim's life could be one way of finding a different job. It would be perfect, I said to myself with great excitement, to do a job which I also enjoyed doing. I felt as hopeful as in those early days when I first met Ruth and considered myself a film-maker. Those were rare moments and I started thinking of Ruth, of the beginning of our relationship. I thought of her with great affection; I hadn't thought of her this way for a long time. Indeed, I remembered how I'd left her that very morning, how in spite of our frank discussion the night before, regretfully this morning, I behaved as if she wasn't there, as if she didn't exist. I'd got up, had a shower, got dressed, had coffee and left the flat without exchanging more than a few dead words with her. It was the simple question, "Do you want to use the shower now?" to which she replied, "You can go first." And that was it.

Now, when I recalled our early life together and compared it with what had been happening lately, I regretted not trying hard enough to make it work, to make Ruth happy. I felt so affectionate towards her that I decided to phone and tell her that in spite of all our difficulties I still loved her. Better still, I would go home and tell her how much I still loved her.

I went home, but to my annoyance Ruth wasn't there.

"Typical!" I said, infuriated, "She's never around when I need her, damn her!" But I managed to control my temper. Rather than waiting for her in this mood I thought I'd better do something useful. I took out my sketch book and started drawing scenes of the proposed film. I drew and drew, cutting off the sheets of the sketches from the book and laying them out on the floor in a sequenced order. I enjoyed doing what I was doing and before long the sitting-room floor was strewn with sketches. I was so excited and thought that would be a great surprise for Ruth. I poured myself a drink and sat waiting for her to turn up. I could just imagine the effect of these sketches on her face. Surely she would be as happy as I was, surely she would be reminded of the old days, and of the happiness and hopes that we had and we would feel happy again. I was happy and wanted Ruth to share my happiness.

Ruth didn't come home until the evening. By then I was exhausted and had fallen asleep on the sofa. When I woke up I had a slight headache, the sense of excitement which I'd entertained in the afternoon was gone.

Ruth was standing there, not as happily astonished as I'd wished her to be, but still looking with some amusement at the sketches covering the floor. She knew that they were sketches for a film, but she couldn't tell what the film was about: they were vague, some not quite finished, and, to be honest, they were badly drawn.

"Can't you guess?" I asked joyfully trying to revive my earlier sense of excitement.

She shook her head.

"It's Salim's story!" I said and went on, telling her what had happened that morning and how I came to think of making this film.

The look of amusement on her face was replaced by one of contempt.

"Your friend is ruining his life and the only thing you can think of is to make a film about him," she looked at me scornfully.

"He's not ruining his life," I started to say and wanted to

add that she had no right to describe his choice as self-destructive. True, that till that morning, I too had thought Salim was walking into self-destruction but now I realised I was wrong. I wanted to explain that he was only doing what would make his life meaningful, but I didn't. The contempt on her face reminded me of the night I was informed that my father had died. It was that look which made me realise, that nothing I said would make her less upset and disgusted. She didn't even want to listen to my excuses. She turned and walked into the bedroom locking the door behind her in a way that made the lock click noisily – just as she did when I told her that I wasn't going to my father's funeral. Locking the door that way wasn't meant to prevent me from going into the room, Ruth knew there was a spare set of keys in the drawer of the kitchen table: rather, the noisy click of the lock was meant to inform me that she didn't want me lying by her side, certainly not that night, and possibly not for the next few. It was a punishment which I had to accept without protest.

Stretching out on the sofa in the sitting room, I found myself reliving that moment on the bus recalling the memories of those days. I understood why Salim might prefer to listen to religious people rather than to any of his friends. He needed someone to talk to him in a way that would reach his heart; he needed to hear a soothing voice which none of his friends could muster. I realised that I had no chance against such a voice and more significantly, I knew that I had no right to stop him listening to that voice. And it was then I realised that a wide gap now separated Salim and me; a gap which I couldn't bridge, nor should I. When, however, I tried to explain this to Ruth the next morning, it didn't sound so convincing.

"You see, Salim wasn't such a close friend of mine." Ruth listened to me reluctantly. "I wanted to believe that he was a close friend. I tried to help him, to save him but all I was doing was trying to convince myself that I actually cared about him being a close friend."

"Or perhaps you were feeling guilty because you tried to fuck his wife," she interrupted me, sarcastically.

"What?" I cried out. I was surprised and annoyed, "You don't understand!"

"Yes, I do."

"No, you don't. I'm trying to explain to you how I felt and you come back with this nasty remark."

"Well, it's true, isn't it?"

I said nothing. I felt like getting up, walking over to her and smacking her, smacking her twice, three times, smacking and kicking her, the bitch!

19

First Sharon visited Haram al-Sharif, then the second intifada started, then I wanted to reveal to Ruth what had happened to Maryam. Instead we fought.

So now I come to the end, to what happened two days ago.

It all started badly. I woke up troubled by the nightmare I'd had. I'd dreamt of Salim standing in the glaring sun, dressed in a mujahedeen outfit. He looked sad and let down. But it wasn't only Salim I dreamt of. There were also Brother Fadi and Cousin Maryam. Fadi was arguing with Father and Uncle Ahmad. It seemed that he was due to leave on a military mission while Father and Uncle Ahmad were begging him not to go. I had had the same dream about Cousin Maryam many times before but this time Salim and Fadi were entangled in what became one long nightmare.

Ruth noticed my disturbed mood but didn't say anything, and I wondered about telling her. I thought I should wait till later in the day to ask her out for dinner perhaps and then tell her about those disturbing dreams. That was the best way to go about it and I went to work feeling less uneasy.

There was very little to do at the magazine, but I was in no mood to work anyway. I left the office and wandered the streets pretending to look for a present for Ruth.

Something was obviously still worrying me, something that made me realise that I couldn't, after all, tell her anything. I couldn't tell her about the nightmares simply because I didn't have the courage to mention Maryam again. Since the time I told her the unconvincing story of Maryam's disappearance and she, understandably enough, got suspicious, I hadn't mentioned my cousin's name again.

No, I couldn't talk to Ruth about the nightmares or about anything else. All day long I felt terrible about both the nightmares and my lack of courage in revealing the secret about Maryam to Ruth. I had to talk to Ruth, I must tell her, I thought, but when eventually I found the courage to do so, I chose the worst possible moment.

We had just learned the terrible news of Sharon's visit to Haram al-Sharif and of the ensuing clashes between Palestinians and Israelis. We were watching it on the television, silently. There was nothing unfamiliar about our silence; we had been watching the news silently for nearly two months, since the end of the Camp David talks. We had felt that nothing further could be said. It's not that we expected the Camp David talks to reach an agreement. We had given up on the possibility of Palestinians and Israelis reaching an agreement months before. The two sides were simply rotten and certainly incapable of agreeing on anything. We reached this conclusion and after that we either watched the news mutely or avoided watching it all together. But with such devastating news as Sharon's visit to Haram al-Sharif, Ruth couldn't help it, she couldn't keep silent that night.

"Why doesn't someone shoot the bastard!" she cried out. "Why doesn't some fucking suicide bomber blow himself and Sharon up instead of blowing up school children."

"Why?" I asked, irritated after waiting for any chance to express my frustration, "Why? Is it because he's revealing who we really are?"

"What are you on about now?" She didn't understand why I was so upset with her, "Who do you believe we are? Sharon? Are you mad?"

"Yes, Sharon," I shouted, getting more agitated, "we are Sharon, we'd rather keep fighting than live together. War is easier than peace, we all know that but only Sharon has the honesty to say so and act accordingly!"

"You are really mad!" She was furious. She was so furious that I thought that she was as ready for a fight as I was.

"You are just a hypocrite!" I replied. "A hypocrite like the rest of your peace-loving friends!"

"Me? A hypocrite? And how about you? Aren't you a hypocrite and a coward too?"

"Shut up!" I screamed, slapping her across the face. "Shut up, you fucking bitch!" I hit her again and again.

Furious, but also terrified, she pushed me so forcefully that I nearly fell over backwards. She jumped up and shot into the bedroom. But before she managed to lock herself in, I pushed the door open. I was trembling with rage, "Coward! Yes, coward, from a family of cowards, a family with no honour!" I shouted hysterically, standing right by the bed. Now I felt that I'd gained the courage

I needed to tell her the true story of Maryam.

"Yes, coward, we are all cowards! That's why Maryam was killed. Yes, you are right, she was killed, not for the sake of our honour, but because we had no honour!"

She stared at me with a mixture of anger, fear and curiosity on her face. I was seething with rage, but no, I said to myself, I must do this properly, I don't want her to be frightened while I'm telling her what happened, I must tell her the story calmly, I must control myself. And I started to calm myself down. I took a deep breath and sat on the edge of the bed, staring silently at the wall. "You want to know what happened, don't you?" I asked, trying my best to sound as composed as I possibly could, "you've always wanted to know what my family did to Maryam. I'll tell you now!"

"You've gone mad!" she screamed. "Get out! Get out right now!"

"But don't you really want to know?"

"Get out!" she screamed again. "Get out or I'll call the police!"

"What?" I was shocked. I understood why she was angry; I understood that she was still frightened because of my fit of rage, but I didn't expect her to be so frightened that she would actually threaten me with the police.

For a moment I wondered how serious she was but I could see that not only was she serious, she looked different too. She looked more like a stranger, a frightened stranger. I couldn't believe it. What had happened to her? How could she have changed so quickly?

"Get out, now!" she shouted again and again.

Stunned, I left the room without looking at her and immediately after I had gone she locked the door, causing that click which had come to signal the end of our arguments. Indeed it had become a sign of an unresolved argument: we argued, she went into the bedroom and I slept on the sofa in the sitting room.

However, this time the clicking was more annoying than on previous occasions. It was too quick and unfair of her to declare the end of our fight, and I nearly turned and reminded her that there was no point in locking the door because there was another key in the drawer of the kitchen table. But I thought I'd better not frighten her any further, that I should wait until she'd calmed down and come out of the bedroom. Deep down, however, I knew she wouldn't. Recalling the look on her face, I realised that she wouldn't come out of the bedroom unless she wanted to get out of the flat and leave for good. True, she wasn't that sort of person, but now after what had happened, she might come to the conclusion that she must leave right away. Perhaps that's exactly what she was planning right now. I instantly decided to get out of her way, to get out of the flat and give her the chance to leave. And I left, slamming the front door behind me so she would know that I'd gone out, that it was safe for her now to come out and do what she'd decided to do.

I went to the local pub, ordered a large scotch and sat at a table in the corner. I was still shocked. I tried to figure out what had got into her, what made her so frightened. But, I said to myself, I should start by asking myself what had got into me too? True, this was not the first time that I'd lost my temper, but it was the first time that I'd ever hit her. My loss of temper now didn't lead only to verbal violence, but physical too. And I knew how much she detested physical violence, especially violence directed against women. How could I have forgotten that?

Very easily. I came to this conclusion after a few minutes' thought, very easily because I'd never actually taken her point of view seriously. I'd always thought of it as feminist rubbish, though I'd never said so to her face. Even now, after all that had happened back home, I didn't seem to take it any more seriously. And what had happened exactly? I had confirmed her worst fears; I swore at her, I hit her and chased her into the bedroom and told her that my cousin Maryam had been killed. No, hitting her was not the only thing that made her so frightened, no, it was the confirmation of her suspicions, of her fear that Maryam had been killed, that she had been the victim of honour-killing. That for her rated as the most extreme form of male violence against women.

What did I expect? I hit her and then tell her that my cousin was killed. But, I wondered, how would she have reacted if she really knew the truth? If she knew that Maryam was a victim of something worse than honour-killing? I imagined Ruth hearing the truth. No, I should think of Maryam, yes, of Maryam.

To hell with Ruth, yes to hell with her, that self-pitying bitch. Maryam is the victim, the ultimate victim whom we all, the whole family of uncles, aunts, and cousin's, claimed had disappeared. She disappeared, we told people, and soon we ourselves believed the lie.

It was nearly a year after brother Fadi was killed. Maryam was sixteen or seventeen. She was not so attractive that men lusted after her, but she was a bright student and very sociable. One day she came home in a state of shock. She couldn't explain what had happened to her but it didn't take her parents, Uncle Khalil and Aunt Aisha, long to guess. We all guessed; she'd been raped.

"Who did that to you?" they wanted to know.

"Who did it?" they actually interrogated her but she couldn't utter a word. Her mother undressed her, washed her and put her to bed. For two days Maryam said nothing and ate nothing, she just remained in bed, weeping.

Uncle Khalil informed Uncle Mohammad, the eldest of my uncles, and he summoned the whole family. A doctor too was brought in to examine her. Of course there was nothing the doctor could tell them that they didn't already know: she'd been raped and she was still in shock. But the family wanted to know who the perpetrator was.

"I swear to God the moment I know the name of the bastard who's done this I shall tear him limb from limb!" my uncle Ahmad swore. He was the youngest and the keenest among my family to get into fights. He was so angry that he paced up and down the front room in which the whole family had gathered. Suddenly he burst into the room where Maryam was resting. He demanded the name of the perpetrator. He hit her. He kept hitting her until she burst into tears. Then there was silence, we could hear nothing. For Uncle Ahmad it must have been the silence of the surprised.

And then we heard him ask, "Are you sure it was him?" He sounded more frightened than sceptical. It wasn't that he didn't believe her but it sounded as if he would rather it had been anyone but him.

"Yes, yes!" and she started sobbing loudly.

He came out, pale faced.

"Who was it?" Uncle Khalil and Aunt Aisha asked, expecting the worst. And when he told them, they too looked more frightened than angry as did everybody else in the room. The perpetrator, it was eventually revealed, was Jalal, a young troublemaker who was well known in the camp. But it wasn't him that my uncles were frightened of. It was his family. Jalal belonged to a big family with members in high positions within Fatah. To shoot him, as Uncle Ahmad swore to do, was to declare war not only on a big family but possibly on Fatah itself. None of my family belonged to a militia or a political organisation and so there was no possibility of our having military backing. Uncle Ahmad knew a few people in various factions, including Fatah itself, but none of them was in an influential enough position to compete with Jalal's uncles and cousins.

When Jalal attacked people, which he quite often did, the victims, or their families, didn't go after him for fear of his family. What they did, however, was to complain to his parents, or uncles and cousins. Complaining to Jalal's family must have crossed my uncles' minds – apart perhaps from Uncle Ahmad – but this assault was an assault on our honour and in such cases families of the victim were expected either to punish the perpetrator or force him to marry the girl whose honour he'd abused, or as a last resort, hope that nobody would find out. My uncles couldn't punish Jalal, but neither could they go to his family demanding that he marry Maryam. No responsible family wanted Jalal marrying their daughter. Of course nobody cared what Maryam wanted or thought. She was the victim, true, but an embarrassing victim and there were times when physical pain and shame caused her to sob hysterically and she was told to shut up and stop causing more embarrassment. Some uncles talked about her as if she were to blame.

"What's the matter with you?" Uncle Ahmad shouted at them. And then he muttered to himself as if he wasn't sure what to do, "Are you frightened of him now? Do we do nothing? Do we let him tread all over our honour and do nothing? We must get the bastard!"

"But that could mean bloodshed," Uncle Mohammad replied.

"You are right!' agreed Uncle Khalil. Though the matter primarily concerned his daughter, it wasn't surprising to hear Uncle Khalil agreeing with Uncle Mohammad. Uncle Mohammad was the eldest and therefore his opinion must be respected but Uncle Khalil was also frightened of causing a bloody fight with another family because of what had happened to his daughter. Uncle Khalil was known as a peaceful man, a term which quite often meant a coward.

"Do we forget it then?" Uncle Ahmad asked defiantly.

"For now, yes, we forget it," Uncle Mohammad said, obviously preferring that we keep quite though pretending to imply otherwise. "We do nothing until the time comes when we can make that bastard pay without getting our family in a war with his."

It sounded a good idea. They all agreed including Uncle Ahmad, who at first was reluctant. "I shall be counting every minute until the time comes when we can get that bastard Jalal!" although he sounded as if he was only trying to hide his embarrassment for backing off so easily.

The problem, however, didn't disappear. Five weeks later, Aunt Aisha discovered that Maryam was pregnant. The whole family gathered again to discuss what to do. After much talking and arguing, Uncle Mohammad came up with the suggestion that Maryam should be sent away to some distant relatives living in Beirut. They should be told that she was married but that her husband had just died. That should explain the shameful fact of being pregnant without having a husband.

Apart from Uncle Ahmad, everybody thought that was a good idea. "And when she gives birth, what do we do? Bring up a bastard?"

"Let's hope that by then we have found her a husband," Uncle Mohammad replied.

Uncle Ahmad didn't seem convinced but said nothing for a while. When he spoke again, he said he should be the one to take Maryam to Beirut. He was the only one who had a car. Uncle Khalil and Aunt Aisha exchanged worried looks but didn't say anything. Maryam's fate was left to Uncle Ahmad whose behaviour was becoming increasingly erratic.

Early the next morning, Maryam was pushed into the back seat of Uncle Ahmad's car. She was weeping bitterly. Her mother was crying too. Uncle Ahmad was angry and told them to shut up otherwise he would shoot them both. He got in and drove away speedily.

That was the last we saw of Maryam. Uncle Ahmad himself didn't come back until the evening. Everybody, especially Uncle Khalil and Aunt Aisha, had been worried sick and when he eventually turned up they looked anything but relieved.

"The look on his face," Aunt Aisha said, describing Uncle Ahmad, "was similar to Maryam's on the day she was assaulted."

For days Uncle Ahmad was completely distracted. Whatever was said to him had to be repeated several times before he took it in. A week later he packed his clothes and left. He went to Beirut, remained there for a short while then left the country altogether. Nobody knew where he had gone. Some claimed that he went to Germany, others said that he was living somewhere in Latin America.

Uncle Ahmad didn't say what exactly he did to Maryam but almost everybody knew. Those of us who didn't, came to realise the truth when, just a couple of days before he left for good, we heard him ordering Aunt Aisha to stop crying; she had been crying ever since Uncle Ahmad had returned in such a state.

"Stop crying or I'll bury you with her!" he threatened.

After Uncle Ahmad left nobody mentioned Maryam again. Everybody agreed that she had disappeared and nobody knew where she was.

Cold-blooded cowards! That's what we were, what we are, I said to myself, while sitting in the pub recalling Maryam's tragedy. I must tell Ruth everything. I'll go back now and tell her. I must be honest with her and tell her everything, as it happened without any omissions, but deep down I knew that there was no point. Ruth no longer wanted to know. She was frightened and the only thing she wanted, the only thing she was thinking right now, was that she must get out, run away and disappear.

Yes, that's what she wants to do, leave me – and now I couldn't help thinking that she wasn't leaving me because she was frightened, no, she wanted to leave me because she'd found someone else. She'd found herself a man and she was leaving me for his sake, I thought, jealous and angry. This whole episode, her being terrified of me, threatening me with the police, it's only a ploy to make a justifiable exit. She only wanted to move in with her lover.

Yes, I convinced myself, she was leaving me not because she was frightened but because she had committed an act of treason, and a traitor must be killed. I'll kill her if she leaves me! I said to myself and got up determining to go home and confront her. But I didn't go home straight away, instead I went to the bar and bought myself another drink.

20

First Ruth moved in with me, then we thought of having a baby, then my father died. But now she's gone out and I'm sitting here recalling the last seven years of my life, from the first time we met until what happened two days ago.

Ruth's gone to the post office. I've been waiting for her for two days now. I've been sitting here on the sofa, in the sitting room, since the evening before last when I came back from the pub and tried to tell her what happened to Maryam. I'd expected her to have taken advantage of my absence and be gone. But to my relief I discovered that she hadn't. I didn't want her to leave.

I thought of knocking on the bedroom door to say that I needed to talk to her, to open my heart to her, or at least to thank her for not abandoning me. But I was worried that she might still be angry, or even frightened. The fact that she hadn't left the flat in my absence didn't necessarily mean that she'd calmed down. I thought of waiting until the morning but knew that I couldn't sleep before I'd talked to her. I decided to use the spare key to open the door quietly, and before she got the chance to protest, kneel in front of her, begging her to listen to me.

I went to the kitchen and opened the drawer where the spare set of keys was always kept. To my astonishment it wasn't there. I had seen the keys only a couple of days before, where could have they gone? I searched for them on the shelves and in the cupboards, when eventually it dawned on me: she'd taken them. In my absence, she came out of the bedroom and took the spare keys to prevent me from entering the room. Now I knew for sure that she was still frightened of me. I couldn't believe that after living with me, sleeping with me, eating with me, for five years, she was really so frightened of me. I could no longer remain calm and went and knocked at the bedroom door.

"Go away!" Her voice came clear and as determined as before.

"I need to talk to you."

"Not now, tomorrow!" she replied firmly.

"I need to talk to you now!" I shouted, my irritation increasing.

"Go away!" she shouted again, "Go away, or I'll call the police!"

The police, again! The bitch is still threatening me with the police! Furious as I was, I couldn't hold back the sarcasm: "Well if you really want to call the police then you have to come out here where the telephone is! Or would you like me to call them for you? Ha! You fucking bitch!" and with the strength that comes with anger I kicked the door, once, twice, and flung it wide open. She jumped up and rushed towards me, no doubt hoping to push past me, but I blocked her way out so her only option was to confront me. She started hitting me, screaming and hitting me. At first I tried to stop her screaming. It was midnight and I was worried that the neighbours would hear her. With one hand I got hold of the back of her neck and pressed the palm of my other hand over her mouth: "Shut up! Shut up or I'll kill you!" I threatened.

Her face was so pale and those brown eyes which I'd adored, especially when washed with tears, were wide with terror. I couldn't help feeling a sense of satisfaction.

She didn't give in though. She started scratching my face, trying to reach my eyes with her finger nails. I took my hand off her mouth and seized her neck from the front; her neck was now encircled by my hands.

No longer gagged and her voice hoarse, she croaked, "You're a bastard! You fucking Arab terrorist!" But I could no longer hear or see her.

This wasn't Ruth, this was some stranger trying to scratch my eyes out. I tightened my grip around her neck. This wasn't Ruth – Ruth's gone. I had seen her minutes earlier carrying a parcel and going out. I squeezed harder and harder until the hands that had been trying to get at my eyes fell away; the arms swung against the side of the body, the stranger's body. I let go and the body fell on the carpeted floor with a thud. I left it there and walked into the sitting room.

Now I'm sitting here, watching a black and white film, recollecting my life over the past seven years and finishing my breakfast; the fried eggs with pitta bread and fresh vegetables, the strong smell and taste of fresh spring onions are all around me. I have been sitting here for two days now. I have been waiting for Ruth. She has gone to the post office.